Her warm scent surrounded him, filling Frank's head with all sorts of imaginings better left for late nights and soft beds.

Angel kept a firm hold on his handcuffed wrist. "Let's see if we can do this nice and easy. Swing your legs out of the car, stand up and turn around."

He followed her directions. She was close enough that he could feel her warm breath fanning the exposed skin of his throat. Close enough that he could see her swallow and watch the dawning awareness in her eyes.

Close enough that she would notice exactly how…aware…he was in a couple of seconds.

If he didn't watch out, this attraction would get out of hand way too easily. He'd already broken one of his rules by talking to a civilian about his assignment.

He stood dangerously close to breaking a few more.

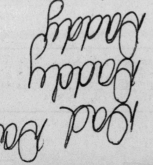

Dear Reader,

Winter may be cold, but the reading's hot here at Silhouette Intimate Moments, starting with the latest CAVANAUGH JUSTICE tale from award winner Marie Ferrarella, *Alone in the Dark*. Take one tough cop on a mission of protection, add one warmhearted veterinarian, shake, stir, and...voilà! The perfect romance to curl up with as the snow falls.

Karen Templeton introduces the first of THE MEN OF MAYES COUNTY in *Everybody's Hero*—and trust me, you really will fall for Joe Salazar and envy heroine Taylor McIntyre for getting to go home with him at the end of the day. FAMILY SECRETS: THE NEXT GENERATION concludes with *In Destiny's Shadow*, by Ingrid Weaver, and you'll definitely want to be there for the slam-bang finish of the continuity, not to mention the romance with a twist. Those SPECIAL OPS are back in Lyn Stone's *Under the Gun*, an on-the-run story guaranteed to set your heart racing. Linda O. Johnston shows up *Not a Moment Too Soon* to tell the story of a desperate father turning to the psychic he once loved to search for his kidnapped daughter. Finally, welcome new author Rosemary Heim, whose debut novel, *Virgin in Disguise*, has a bounty hunter falling for her quarry—with passionate consequences.

Enjoy all six of these terrific books, then come back next month for more of the best and most exciting romance reading around—only from Silhouette Intimate Moments.

Enjoy!

Leslie J. Wainger
Executive Editor

Please address questions and book requests to:
Silhouette Reader Service
U.S.: 3010 Walden Ave., P.O. Box 1325, Buffalo, NY 14269
Canadian: P.O. Box 609, Fort Erie, Ont. L2A 5X3

Virgin in Disguise

ROSEMARY HEIM

Silhouette®

INTIMATE MOMENTS™

Published by Silhouette Books

America's Publisher of Contemporary Romance

SILHOUETTE BOOKS

ISBN 0-373-27402-5

VIRGIN IN DISGUISE

Copyright © 2004 by Rosemary Heim

Visit Silhouette Books at www.eHarlequin.com

Printed in U.S.A.

ROSEMARY HEIM

grew up on a dairy farm, attended a one-room school-house, lived in an English castle and (finally) settled in Minneapolis. She lives in a charming old house (which needs much work) with her romantic husband (who doesn't need much work at all) and four cats (who work very hard at being cute).

Rosemary would love to hear from readers. You can visit her Web site at www.rosemaryheim.com or write to her c/o Midwest Fiction Writers, P.O. Box 24107, Minneapolis, MN 55424.

To Elise Heim and Dorothy Bentler.
My mother and sister. Special women, both.

ACKNOWLEDGMENTS

My heartfelt thank-yous to:
Shannon Godwin, for believing in Angel's story
and being our champion. Dr. Lou Betty Rood and
members of KOD for coming to my medical assistance,
pointing me in the right direction and letting me know
I was on the right track. The Princesses and my critique
group, a phenomenal collection of women. You know
why. And Georgie-Peaux. I miss your calls, long talks
and friendship. The state fair will never be the same.

Author's note to those familiar with downtown
Minneapolis—I know. Please forgive my artistic
license in relocating an escalator or two and
building the library before its time.

Chapter 1

"There ya go, darlin'," the thick southern-accented voice coaxed. "Wake up and let me see those baby blues."

Frank Cabrini did not want to open his eyes—no matter how gentle and enticing that voice sounded. If he did, the light would just set off another set of drums to join the timpani already pounding a rhythm in his brain.

A gentle hand smoothed through his hair, sliding down to pat his cheek. The faint scent of vanilla surrounded him. His eyelids flickered against his will.

"Are you sure he's going to be okay?" Another woman's voice registered in his fuzzy brain.

"Sure. Thanks for your help." The first voice again, this time without the southern inflections. "Go ahead and take off. I can handle things from here."

Frank fought the fog muffling his awareness. Something was wrong. Way wrong. He didn't recognize either voice. The last thing he could remember was sipping a tonic water at the shabby CC Club bar and being chatted up by a woman who looked better suited to lunch at Chino Latino, the trendy Minneapolis Uptown restaurant.

That was how long ago?

Now, he lay stretched out on a bed that wasn't his. He could tell because it was too short for his six-foot-four frame, and the pillow under his head was flat as Nebraska.

Somewhere to his left, a door clicked shut. He wanted to ask what was going on, but his mouth felt like the morning after cleaning out the liquor cabinet.

Vanilla surrounded him again as his head was lifted and something pressed against his lips. Water, cool and unflavored, dribbled into his mouth.

"Thanks." His voice cracked on the single word. The bed shifted and the vanilla scent faded. He turned his head and tried opening his eyes. He knew better than to leave himself vulnerable like this. In his line of work, it could get you dead real fast.

Whatever drug he'd been slipped was wearing off. The water helped clear his head, but his arms and legs still felt weighed down with lead.

He pried his eyes open a slit, just enough to let in a little light. Not that the heavily curtained windows allowed much to filter into the room. What he could see was mostly shadows.

The bed dipped again, creaking with the movement. The woman leaned over him to brush the hair away from his face with one hand. Her other hand slid down his arm, pausing a moment to test his biceps before continuing down to his hand. He watched with a detachment he blamed on the drug as she raised his arm above his head.

Something cool and hard pressed against his wrist, accompanied by the sound of metal sliding through a ratchet. *Handcuffs.* A surge of adrenaline cleared the last of the drug's effects from his system, and his eyes snapped open.

The first thing he saw was the cold gray barrel of a gun. Second were the colder gray eyes of the woman holding him at gunpoint. Instinct had him jerking his shackled arm, trying to get free.

"Don't bother." She spoke with the non-accent of a network newscaster now.

Holy hell, he was in some sort of trouble. "Your accent slipped."

"Well, like, duh," she said, snapping an imaginary wad of chewing gum as she slid into Valley Girl. "As if I'd give you a clue."

The bed squeaked as she stood. Frank followed the lines of her lean body as she straightened, the gun still held steady and pointed right at him.

She was tall. He flicked a glance downward but couldn't see if shoes augmented the impressive height. He doubted it. From the way she carried herself, he didn't see anything artificial or out of balance in her posture.

Her clothes were nothing special—worn blue jeans and a too-big navy-blue T-shirt. A wide, black leather belt wrapped around her waist, held in place with a wicked-looking flattened spike. Dark hair pulled away from her face. No jewelry, not even a watch, interrupted the clean lines of her hands and arms. If she wore makeup, it was minimal and unnoticeable.

A memory wavered into being. He recognized her from the bar. She'd been sitting alone at a corner booth. "You were following me?"

She raised one straight eyebrow, but didn't answer.

Instead, she squatted beside the bed. She worked her free hand beneath him, wriggled her fingers into his left back pocket and pulled out his wallet.

Relief eased the tension in his muscles. Seemed like a lot of work to go through just to rob him, but this kind of trouble he could manage. At least his cover wasn't blown.

His jailer settled into the straight-back chair next to the bed. She laid the snub-nosed revolver in her lap and began to rifle through the contents of his wallet. It wouldn't take long.

"I don't carry credit cards. You're welcome to what cash there is, but it sure don't seem worth all this effort."

She pulled out the driver's license. The bogus name, Frank Boylen, went with his cover story, and would lead to a fabricated history if she tried to dig.

She tossed the wallet onto the mattress beside him, but kept the license. Holding it between two fingers, she tilted it from side to side, then inspected the back before flipping it to land neatly on top of the wallet. She picked up her gun and pointed it back at him. "So, Frank Cabrini, anything you want to tell me before I haul your butt in and collect my bounty?"

Bounty? Oh, hell.

Three facts registered as new tension threaded cold fingers along his spine.

His captor was a bounty hunter.

She knew his real name.

He was in a world of trouble.

Angela Marie Donovan, aka Angel, studied her prisoner's reaction. Background information had included that little tidbit about the license being under a false name.

Whoever Frank Cabrini was, he was good at the game. His only reaction to her use of his real name had been a slight widening of his eyes and the involuntary dilation of his pupils. The muscles in his arm flexed as he tested the handcuffs, but his movements were subtle. He didn't struggle.

Memory of the strength she'd felt in those muscles warmed her hand. Her reaction to this transient bothered her. He wasn't her type. Not that she had a type, much to the chagrin of well-meaning friends. But this guy was even further out of sync than the last blind date her friend Tina had set up for her.

No, Frank Cabrini was so rough she could file her nails on his edges. His black hair was in desperate need of a cut. Either that, or it needed another month or two of growth before he'd be able to tie it away from his face.

What she could see of his face piqued her curiosity. Blue eyes, the same color as the Minnesota summer sky, studied her with a clarity that might unnerve a weaker soul. Especially when contrasted with the heavy beard that hadn't been groomed or trimmed in a longer period of time than his hair.

In general, his appearance fairly shouted, "Danger! Stay away!"

His appearance did, but not his manner. She'd watched him at the bar. No one approached him, but he'd been civil enough to the bartender and waitress. When Tina had sidled up to him, he'd acknowledged her, but he hadn't hit on her. He'd played the gentleman, right up to the moment the sedative had kicked in and they wrestled his semiconscious butt up the stairs to this makeshift holding cell.

Cabrini rattled the handcuff against the old wrought-iron headboard. "Is this really necessary?"

"For now."

"Care to tell me what this is all about?"

She smiled. He was cool enough about the whole situation—she'd give him that. Most men took exception to being handcuffed. At least, they did when it was without prior consent.

Cabrini's calm didn't fit the profile of the typical collar.

After almost ten years in the business of tracking down bail jumpers, she had a pretty good sense of the norm. Cabrini differed from her usual quarry, both because of his manner and because of her client.

She decided to indulge a little curiosity. "Now Mistah Cabrini, suh." She slid back into the southern accent. It usually elicited the most information. "Just what did you go and do to get yourself into this predicament, hmm?"

His eyes narrowed and he took his sweet time answering. No skin off her. She could outwait him any day.

"If you really are a bounty hunter—"

"We in the industry prefer 'bail bond enforcer.'"

He shifted on the bed and rolled onto his side, probably trying to get more comfortable. Good luck.

"Regardless of what you call yourself, don't you normally inquire as to the nature of the criminal you're hunting?"

She nodded, conceding the point. "I always find it entertaining to hear the tales of woe spun out as an excuse for bad behavior."

"Sorry to disappoint you, sweetheart. No sad tale here. In fact, I can't begin to imagine why you think there's a bounty on my head." He shrugged, an oddly elegant gesture in spite of his awkward position. "Who sent you on this fool's chase, anyway?"

She shook her head. "I'm sorry, but that is privileged information. My client prefers to remain anonymous, at least for the time being."

Cabrini rolled onto his back and scooted into a sitting position with his back braced against the wall. The new position had them on the same level, looking eye to eye. "We seem to be at something of an impasse. You won't divulge your client's name, and I can't think of any bail I've jumped, nor anyone who would want me bad enough to send a bou—bail bond enforcer after me."

"Well, suh, you'll just have to ponder a bit harder. Perhaps it will come to you." She stood, regaining the dominant position and forcing him, once again, to look up at her. "I'll leave you to your musings."

"You'll be back?" The faintest hint of concern threaded through his voice.

She smiled and sashayed to the door, paused and glanced over her shoulder at him. "Rest your poor, troubled head, Mistah Cabrini. I shall return with all due haste." With one last hip sway, she pulled the door closed behind her.

The southern-belle facade disappeared with her next step. She reverted to her natural stride, tucking her Smith & Wesson Airweight into her back waistband as she moved the few steps to the end of the hall. From that vantage point, she could watch the street below while keeping an eye on the door to the room, as well as the stairs leading down to the street. The metal fire escape outside the window would allow for a quick departure if that became necessary.

This was as close to privacy as she was going to get for a while. She pulled out her cell phone and scrolled through the address book. She needed to sort through a few details.

She'd known her client, Marvin Dexter, her entire life. Honorary uncle and surrogate father since her dad's death, when he'd approached her about tracking down Cabrini, she'd made an exception to her "no family" rule. It was the least she could do after all the ways Dex had helped over the years

And if that wasn't enough motivation, her mother's health insurance had gone up again. The extra money she earned for bringing in Cabrini would go a long way to help cover that bill.

She highlighted a number and punched "ok."

Dex answered on the first ring, his cultured tones clear on the cellular connection.

"Hey, Dex. It's me. I've got him."

"Already?" The question followed a brief pause. "I hadn't expected you to catch up with him so soon."

"Yeah, well, I'm just that good. Which is why you hired me, right? Now that I've got him, do you want me to bring him down to your office?"

"No." Another pause, longer this time, which was out of character for Dex. He was known in his political circles for his sharp intellect and quick responses. "I'm not ready to meet with Mr. Cabrini. There are still a few details I need to iron out."

"What am I supposed to do with him in the meantime? I can't very well keep him locked up in this room."

"I'm sorry, sweetie."

The endearment triggered a tiny ache in her chest. She could hear the echo of her father's voice in the phrase, even after almost twenty years.

"The situation is quite complicated," Dex continued, "and everything needs to be right before we can proceed."

"You didn't tell me there was a timing issue."

"I know, and I apologize for that omission. Nevertheless, it would be extremely awkward for me to take custody right now."

"Awkward for you? I'm the one with a man in custody and no warrant. Can you at least help me out on that?"

"I don't have anything to take to a judge. At least, not yet."

"I'm skating a thin line here, Dex." She paced the short distance from window to door and back. Working blind did not leave her with a good feeling. "Can you at least give me a clue as to what this is all about?"

"He's been poking around in some old cases." Dex paused, then added in a lowered tone, "Of your father's and mine."

Her throat tightened. "Why would he do that?" She pushed a swallow through the knot. "Do you think he knows something?"

"I really don't want to say any more right now. I need more time. Do you think you could take him out of town for a while?"

"How long?"

"A few days, that's all. You could use my cabin until it's time to bring him back."

Angel weighed the offer, comparing it to other obligations, trying to make this new scenario fit. "I'll need to make a couple stops first, but I think I can work it out."

"Good, good. I'll leave a key with your mother—I assume one of your stops will be there before you leave?"

"Of course."

"Excellent. I'm about to leave my office for a few errands of my own. The key will be there when you arrive, along with some additional information."

"Is there any chance you can get a warrant on him for something?"

"That simply isn't a possibility at this time." Dex's sigh hinted at some annoyance. "Angel?"

"Yes?"

"I can't begin to tell you how much I appreciate your help in this matter. You do understand that, don't you?"

"Of course." Did he understand the risk she was taking for him?

"And you appreciate the need to keep this strictly confidential?"

"I am a professional."

"I meant no insult. This is a delicate project, and you're the only one I can trust to do it."

"Sorry." Angel reined in her momentary irritation. "It's going to take me an hour or two to get things in order. I'll stop at home last, before I leave town." That should give Dex plenty of time to drop off the key.

"What are you going to do with Cabrini until you leave?"

"Good question. I'll figure something out."

"I have every confidence that you will, Angel. You've always impressed me with your resourcefulness. When I have everything lined up here, I'll be in touch with you."

"We'll talk then." Angel closed her cell phone and slid it into her front pocket. Dex wasn't telling her everything, but he was family. She trusted him more than she trusted most. That entitled him to some leeway. She just wished he'd been a bit more forthcoming with information.

He hadn't given her any more than what she already knew—that he wanted Cabrini brought in. There didn't appear to be any legal charges against him, so it was more of a P.I. locate job.

Considering she had Cabrini in custody, in handcuffs, she could probably be charged with kidnapping. It wouldn't be the first time she'd bent the rules to suit the situation. Still, the idea didn't sit well. Comfort came from knowing such a charge would never occur to most of the lowlife types she dealt with.

But then, Frank Cabrini didn't fit that stereotype. He was nothing like she'd expected. The rough exterior he presented was every bit a disguise, same as her faked accents and wigs.

His eyes reinforced the perception that he wasn't what he appeared to be. Clear and steady, his gaze spoke of curiosity and intelligence. He had barely shifted his glance from her since he'd awakened.

Those damned blue eyes seemed to see into her soul. And that, more than anything, unsettled her.

She didn't like the feeling. Not one bit.

Frank tugged at the handcuff. He could probably work his way free, given enough time and a little ingenuity. Ingenuity he could handle, but the time factor was too big of an unknown. He didn't like gambling when the odds were stacked against him.

In the hall, creaking floorboards betrayed the movements of his captor. The murmur of a one-sided conversation leaked through the thin wall. He caught a snatch that sounded a lot like, *Do you think he knows something?*

That finished any thoughts of attempting to escape— he wanted to know who the hell had ordered this bounty. He settled into a slightly more comfortable position and turned his attention to his captor.

First impressions didn't yield much information. That, in itself, told him something. She was no rookie. She hadn't let much slip, other than her accent. Even then, she'd run through so many variations, he couldn't begin to guess what might be normal for her. Lacking that small bit of information prevented his figuring out her background, which could lead to more clues.

The fact that she had his real name could prove problematic. His assignment necessitated a cover story and false identity to work. He'd have to make sure he didn't come in contact with anyone connected to his investigation.

Assuming she wasn't somehow connected already. With no clues to her employer's identity, he wouldn't rule out that possibility.

He swung his legs off the bed and stood. Waves of dizziness threatened to swamp him, and he hung onto the cool metal headboard, taking slow, deep breaths until his balance returned to normal.

Other than leaving him with a faint nausea, the drug seemed to have no lingering effect on his system. He stretched his arms and legs and did a couple of cautious squats. Everything seemed to be in working order, limited only by the very short leash of the handcuff around his wrist.

The door opened. His captor returned, and she was looking none too pleased. When she saw him standing, she pulled her gun from the back of her waistband. She didn't point it at him, which seemed encouraging. She knew how to handle a gun and didn't appear to be trigger happy, just cautious.

"Take your seat, please."

Frank complied, sitting to face her, with both feet on the floor and his free hand on his thigh, palm up. His cuffed hand rested on the pillow, also palm up. He had no intention of doing anything that could be misinterpreted as a threatening gesture.

"What size pants do you wear?"

The question came from so far out in left field, he didn't respond immediately. The information was hardly classified, and there seemed to be no reason not to share it. Then again, he couldn't come up with a logical reason for her query.

"Mind if I ask why you want to know?"

"We're going out of town for a few days, and I figure I better pick up some things to tide you over. You're going to need clothes. No razor, but shampoo, toothbrush…" She continued, adding items to her list.

"Out of town" didn't work for him. Not by a long shot. "It seems like a waste to buy new when we could just go over to my place and pack my own things." If he could talk her into stopping at his place, he could get his hands on—

"Nice try, but neither one of us will be going anywhere near your room."

Room, not apartment or house. She knew how he lived, if not where.

He nodded in understanding. She wasn't going to risk being seen in the rooming house he'd called home for the past two months, with him or without him. "In that case, thirty-four waist, thirty-six inseam. If you're getting jeans, Levi's fit best. I prefer my shirts extra large, tall if you can get them. Otherwise, short-sleeved would be easiest."

She stared at him, one eyebrow raised in disbelief.

"I prefer clothes that fit well." He shrugged, not feeling particularly apologetic.

"I see. Anything else?"

"Yes." A slow grin pulled up one side of his mouth. "Boxers."

Soft color flooded up her neck, darkening her cheeks. Well, well. Now that was interesting.

"It's going to take me a little while to gather everything together." She crossed to the dresser, where a bottle of water and several plastic cups shared space with a battered television with rabbit-ear antennae. She turned on the TV, tuning it to the least static-filled station, and turned the volume to a reasonable level—loud enough to hear, not so loud that any possible neighbors would object.

"My assistant isn't available to keep an eye on you while I'm gone. I can't take any chances right now, so you're going to have to take another sedative."

"I don't think so."

"You really don't have the option of whether or not to take it." She pulled a small dopp kit from the top dresser drawer and opened it. "You can choose how. Either take it orally or I can give you a shot. My recommendation is go for the drink. I've never been very good with needles."

"In that case, line 'em up, barkeep." Orally also held the advantage of being able to regurgitate the sedative once she left.

She emptied two capsules into one of the glasses and filled it with water. So much for plan A. She handed the glass to him then stepped back and waited.

He eyed the mixture, sizing up the quantity of liquid. He could still do this—pretend to swallow, and once she left, spit it out. His system would probably absorb some of the sedative, but not enough to incapacitate him for long. He raised the glass in a mock salute and drained the contents.

"Mistah Cabrini, suh?" She was back to the southern accent. "You may as well go ahead and swallow for real. I won't be leaving until the drug has taken effect."

Ah, hell. He was beginning to hate that southern-belle act. He swallowed.

"Thank you. Now, why don't you rest your weary

head on that pillow and get comfortable. It won't take but a few minutes for you to drift off."

He stretched out on the mattress, tempted to fight the lethargy already beginning to weigh down his limbs, but knowing it would be futile. He folded both hands beneath his head, crossed his ankles and glared at her until he faded into oblivion.

Chapter 2

Angel tossed the bull's-eye-spotted bags in the trunk of her car, glad to have that portion of her list out of the way. The credit gods had been merciful—most of the items she needed were on sale. Better still, these particular charges wouldn't come due until well after she'd received payment for this job.

The car rattled as she slammed the trunk shut, and she gave the dented fender an affectionate pat as she rounded to the driver's door. Old Rusty's body had seen better days, but it served its purpose. Few would guess the dilapidated red shell hid a chassis-and-engine combo that could outrun just about anything on the road. The engine purred to life, and she pulled out of the parking lot.

It didn't take long to reach her last stop, even with a detour through the drive-up ATM. The modest rambler, shaded by several old oak trees, sat back from the quiet street. Traffic cruising past Cedar Lake seldom came down these twisting streets, providing the illusion of seclusion in the middle of Minneapolis.

"Grampa Fred," head of the Neighborhood Watch and honorary grandfather to every kid in a four-block radius, waved as she drove by his corner house. He provided the illusion of continuity and security.

The garage door opened with the touch of a button, and she backed into her space with practiced ease. She slipped through the connecting door into the kitchen and down the stairs to her basement office.

Shedding the wig and contact lenses, she transformed to her "normal" blue-eyed, sorta blond self before heading back to the kitchen. She crunched on baby carrots from the refrigerator as she sifted through the mail. Bills, junk mail, a couple of bank statements.

Not for the first time, she considered consolidating the money into one bank. But the mostly inactive savings account, inherited from her father, provided some emotional touchstone for her mother. That alone made the few extra pieces of paper a minor inconvenience.

"I thought I heard you come in." Corie Anderson, her mother's companion and caretaker, came around the corner from the dining room.

Angel turned and smiled. "Hi, Corie. How is she today?"

"Today was mostly a good day."

"Mostly?"

"She spent much of her time reading a book." Corie crossed to the refrigerator and pulled out a diet pop. "We watched a movie. Then Mr. Dexter stopped by. He left an envelope for you—it's on the front hall table."

"Did he visit with Mom?"

Corie nodded, but a frown shadowed her face.

"What?" Angel prompted.

"She's just been very moody lately. Mostly sad."

Angel looked out the window over the sink. The grass needed mowing again. Already. Had it been a week? Probably longer. She shook her head and pulled back from the momentary escape. "I have to go out of town for a few days. As soon as I finish packing, I'll come in and see if I can get her to talk some."

"I wonder if it's her medication."

"You think she's having a bad reaction?"

"It's not that so much as I don't think this new stuff is as effective as the original prescription."

"Dr. Brenna said it would take some time to transition, and for the new meds to reach optimum levels." She pulled a bottle of spring water from the refrigerator. "Until then, we're bound to see some symptoms of the depression and paranoia."

Corie nodded. "I guess that makes sense. But I keep wondering if maybe you should get a second opinion? I know of another doctor…."

Angel sighed. "I don't know. Between Dr. Sanders all of a sudden disappearing without a word, Mom's files getting lost, finding a new doctor and now this new prescription…it's been a lot of change. At least she seems to like Dr. Brenna."

She exchanged a look with Corie. Her mother's moods had taken a marked downturn nearly two months ago. The change had been difficult for all of them.

Angel held the cool water bottle to her chest, wishing it would soothe the ache building there. She wanted her father, wanted their little family whole. Except some bail jumper— She shook off that line of thought.

"Tell her I'll be in in just a few minutes. It won't take me long to pack."

"Sure."

Angel turned back to the window. "The lawn needs

mowing. You better call a service and get it done. I'm not sure how long I'll be gone."

"I'll take care of it. You pay me enough to do more than sit around all day."

Angel smiled. Since joining their little household two years ago, Corie had become indispensable. "Don't sell yourself short. Having you is a godsend. I don't know how we managed without you."

"Then we saved each other." Corie gave her a quick hug. "If you hadn't exposed my ex for the rat he was, I'd probably be dead now. The best thing I got out of that disastrous marriage was this job."

"Thank Dex for that. He came up with the idea. All I did was make the offer."

"As far as I'm concerned, the offer is all that counts. I'll tell Maryam you're home."

Angel watched the seconds tick off as she drained her bottle of water. Precious time—time spent away from Mom—chasing shadows and ghosts that might not even exist anymore.

The chase was essential, and lately it seemed like she was actually making some headway. She was closer now than she'd ever been to tracking down the arsonist who'd killed her father. If she could keep at it a little longer, she'd succeed. She knew it in her bones.

Then, maybe, she'd capture the person she most needed to find—her mother.

Dropping the empty bottle into the recycling bin, she headed back to the basement. Ten minutes and a change of clothes later, she stowed a small suitcase filled with a range of wardrobe options in Rusty's trunk, along with a gym bag now filled with the clothes and supplies she'd picked up for Cabrini. Another five minutes, and she had her overnight bag packed and sitting by the back door, ready for her departure.

She pulled a pint of Godiva chocolate ice cream from the freezer, grabbed a couple of spoons and headed for the living room.

The afternoon sun wrapped the butter-yellow room in a golden glow. At the center, her mother, dressed in tan slacks and a pale green cotton sweater, sat next to a side table piled with books.

"Hi, Mom." Angel flopped down next to her on the chocolate leather couch and handed her a spoon. "Time for dessert."

"We haven't eaten dinner yet." Her mother's voice held a curious mix of amusement and sadness.

"There's always time for chocolate. You two can do the healthy dinner thing later."

"What about you?" Her mother looked at her with sad, gray eyes.

There had been a time, when Angel was very small, that her mother had laughed all the time. The memories acted as a beacon, reminding Angel of what life could be, would be, someday. If she found her father's killer, her mother could heal and maybe even be happy again.

Angel dug her spoon into the ice cream. "I have to go out of town for a few days. I'm not sure when I'll be back, but I've got my cell phone so you can call me anytime."

"Where are you going?"

"It's nothing to worry about, Mom. I'll be back before you know it."

"When you get back, we should talk."

Angel shot a quick glance at Corie. Corie shrugged and shook her head. "Talk about what?"

Maryam shook her head.

"Do you like your new doctor? Is that what you want to discuss?" Angel tried another tack.

Again, Maryam shook her head, this time casting a furtive glance at her companion.

"Would you prefer to go back to the old medication?"

"No." She picked at the crease of her twill pant leg. "That stuff made me feel…fuzzy, like I'm looking at the world through a big wad of cotton gauze."

"So, the new stuff is better?"

"Better? Yes, but it's still not right. Nothing is right. Nothing's been right since…" She stabbed her spoon into the ice cream.

"I know it was hard to lose Dr. Sanders after all these years. If you don't like Dr. Brenna, we can see about someone else."

"I never trusted that man." Maryam half muttered.

"Who? Dr. Sanders?"

Maryam looked her in the eyes. "It'll be better soon." She smoothed Angel's spiky blond hair away from her face, her hand lingering on her cheek. "You have such beautiful blue eyes. I see your father looking at me every time I look in your eyes."

Tears, hot and unexpected, burned the back of Angel's throat. She bit her lip, fighting the urge to curl into her mother's arms like she was a little girl again. Their roles had reversed too many years ago to go back. Now she needed to be the strong one. The sane one.

Her mother tugged at the short blond hair again. "I wish you'd stop bleaching your hair. And this cut—it's so short and punk. You'd look nice with something more feminine, something like a chin-length bob."

"You know I'm too lazy to spend that much time on my hair." Besides which, short hair fit beneath a wig much better than long hair. Changing identities was easier when she didn't have to worry about her own hair peeking out.

"Where are you going this time?" Her mother switched topics with her usual randomness. Years of practice made it easy for Angel to follow.

"Just up north. I have to take a...friend to a cabin for a little vacation."

"Is that why Marvin came?" Maryam jabbed her spoon into the ice cream again.

"Yes. He asked me to check on his place, since I'm going to be so close."

"I don't think I trust him very much, either."

"Mom, how can you say that? Dex has been a rock for us. Not many men would take on their partner's family as their own."

"Don't judge a book by its cover." Maryam picked up one of the paperbacks in the pile next to her. "I thought this one would be funny. The cover looked funny. But the story was sad."

Angel's head fell back to rest on the couch cushion behind her. Every time they came close to a serious discussion that lasted longer than a few sentences, Maryam drifted off onto another topic.

The antique mantel clock struck the hour and Angel jerked upright. "I need to get going. I'll call you tomorrow, okay?"

"Be careful, sweetie. I need you to come back."

"I know, Mom. I will." She leaned over and pressed a kiss to her mother's soft cheek. "I love you."

Her mother kissed her in turn. "You take such good care of me."

They hugged and Angel stood to leave. Her mother clung to her hand. "You need to stop the bad men." Her voice sounded so fragile and lost.

Angel nodded. "That's what I do, Mom. Stop the bad men." But she hadn't found the one bad man who counted—her father's murderer. She spun on her heel and fled the room before the tears returned. On the way out, she grabbed the key and envelope Dex had left for her.

"Mister, wake up."

Frank groaned. Not again. Didn't he just go through this?

"C'mon, c'mon, c'mon. We don't have much time, we gotta get outta here. Wake up, wake up, wake up."

A slap stung his cheek, followed by a shaking of his shoulders. He shook his head, trying to clear the fog. Definitely different this time. He'd have to be completely unconscious to miss the urgency in this woman's voice.

One of the hands shaking him let go of his shoulder. He covered his head and rolled in anticipation of another slap. The fact that he could move his arm without hindrance registered. The handcuff dangled from his wrist, swinging back and forth when he rolled into a sitting position.

"Can you stand? C'mon, we gotta move. Now."

"Wait a second. What's the rush?" He waved one hand in the air, the other still holding his head against the possibility of falling off—which probably wouldn't be a bad thing, considering how it pounded with each beat of his pulse.

"What d'ya think? We can't stay here."

He pried his eyes open and looked over his shoulder. On the other side of the bed knelt an elf, glaring at him with eyes so blue they couldn't be real. She also had bleached blond hair with an inch of black roots showing and a nose ring.

"Where do you think you're going to take me?"

"Away from here. We'll figure out the details once you're in the car and we're on the road. Now c'mon."

The elf stood. She was very tall for an elf. He shook his head.

Holy hallucinations, he needed his brain back. Until he could think straight, he'd buy a little time and follow his rescuer's urgings. At least he was out of the handcuffs.

He stood, swayed and caught himself on the headboard.

Elf rounded the bed and slipped her arm around his waist, grabbing his belt to support some of his weight. "C'mon."

He draped an arm over her shoulders as she practically dragged him across the room to the door. She paused to peek outside, then pulled him down the hall to the head of the stairs.

"Do you think you can make it down without falling and killing yourself?"

"Yeah." He took a deep breath, clearing his head a little more. A faint scent teased his nose, but he couldn't make a connection that made any sense. Time enough for that later. First things first, and that meant getting out of wherever it was he'd been held.

Leaning against the railing and Elf equally, he managed to get to the bottom of the steps without incident. "See? No problem." He didn't try to repress the foolish grin he shot her way.

She surprised him with a grin of her own, which revealed a dimple in her cheek.

"Told you." He met her gaze and his smiled faded. "You have beautiful eyes. Are they real?"

She chuckled, a husky murmur that sent a shiver of interest streaking down his chest.

"They're real. Rusty's over here."

He stumbled to a halt. "Who's Rusty?" Maybe it would be better if he just parted company with her now, sexy laugh or not. No sense getting tangled up with yet another stranger.

Elf glanced up at him. "Rusty is a what, not a who." She tugged on his belt and got him moving again. They rounded the corner of the building and he spotted a seventies-era Mustang with rusted out spots, a coat hanger for an antenna and a pair of fuzzy, red dice dangling from the rearview mirror.

He looked down at Elf and raised an eyebrow. "Rusty."

"Yepper." She opened the passenger door and pointed. "Hop in."

He eased into the seat. It was a tight fit, but he wasn't about to complain. As long as the bucket of bolts held together, and he got as far away from his kidnapper as he could.

She slammed the door shut. He got his first focused look at her as she trotted around the car to the driver's door. Her cherry-red cropped T-shirt teased the low-riding waist of her rumpled tan cargo pants. Thick-soled sneakers finished the outfit. She looked… "How old are you?"

"Legal and then some in every state." She leaned across him, snagged the passenger seat belt and pulled it across his lap. While she fumbled with the latch, he slumped into the seat, enjoying her closeness and the warm scent of vanilla that clung to her skin.

Memory surfaced just as she settled back into her seat and latched her own seat belt. "Aw, hell." He tried to raise his left arm. The handcuff had him manacled to the frame of the car seat, next to the seat belt buckle. "It's you."

Elf turned the key in the ignition and the engine purred to life. "Perfect timing." She pulled away from the curb.

"That's a matter of opinion."

She shrugged as she turned onto a busy one-way street. "I needed to get you out of there with a minimum of fuss. Your hungover cotton-brain zoned in on the clues it had to work with and produced the desired results. You're here and we're on our way."

"This is kidnapping, you know."

She pulled a pair of sunglasses off the dashboard and slipped them on, hiding behind them.

"False imprisonment." He took another poke at her, testing her level of discomfort.

She turned left onto another busy street. Lyndale, he realized, as they drove past the coffee shop and tattoo parlor. They were headed towards downtown. Maybe she was going to take him to the county jail after all.

"I'm a bail bond enforcer." She enunciated each word. "I've taken you into custody, not kidnapped you." That she didn't like the situation came through loud and clear.

She eased up on the gas as they neared an intersection with a red light. The signal changed to green and she sped up again.

"Except, I've never jumped bail, and you said your client was a private party. That doesn't work so well, does it?"

Traffic slowed in front of them. He spotted a police car parked on the cross street and, for a split second, considered trying to signal for help or trying to overpower her. But he wanted to find out who her client was more than he wanted to escape. At the moment, anyway.

She changed lanes to bypass the backup of cars turning into and out of the Wedge Co-op parking lot, then shifted back into the right lane in time to squeak through a yellow light. They hit the on-ramp to Highway 94, heading east.

"Where are you taking me?"

"I told you earlier, before we left."

"Yeah, well, the last few hours are pretty hazy, thanks to the drug-induced stupor I seem to be in. Why don't you refresh my memory?"

A gap in traffic opened and she changed to the exit lane for Highway 35W north. "My employer didn't expect me to catch up with you quite so quick."

"Gee, I'm sorry I was such an easy mark. If I'd known I was being hunted, maybe I could have made it more of a challenge for you."

She ignored his sarcasm. "He's not ready to meet with you and asked me to take you out of town for a few days, until he has some other details in order."

"If all he wanted was a meeting, why the kidnapping?"

She clenched her jaw. "This isn't a kidnapping."

"You couldn't tell by me." He rattled the handcuff. "From where I'm sitting, it sure feels like one."

She glanced at him but didn't respond.

"Come on, Elf. Give me a good reason, just one, why I don't turn you in for what has got to be a major ethical breach."

This time she glared at him. "Elf?"

That got a rise out of her. He smiled. "It seemed to fit when you were crouched next to the bed. I'll admit, you're a bit tall for an elf, but you're still plenty shorter than I am."

"There is nothing elfish about me."

"I don't know. You've got the pixie haircut, a pointy chin, big eyes. The bleach job and nose ring aren't quite in keeping with the concept, but I'm a tolerant guy and can allow a little creative license in the interpretation."

She snorted—a decidedly unelfish expression.

"Maybe," Frank continued, "if I knew your name, I wouldn't have to make one up for you."

"Angel." The road split, and she shifted lanes again, staying with the northbound traffic.

"Angel. No, I don't think so." Frank looked her over. "What happened to your long, brown hair? And your gray eyes?"

"They served their purpose. As did the auburn curls, the black pageboy, the brown eyes, the green eyes."

A soft whistle escaped his lips. He leaned toward her and studied her features in profile. Satisfied, he nodded and settled back against the seat. "You've been following me for a few days, haven't you?"

"Almost a full week, actually." She flicked a glance in his direction. "You lead a particularly uneventful and rather predictable existence."

"Like I said, if I'd known I was being hunted, I could have made it a little more interesting." A week. And he hadn't spotted her. Even if he wasn't expecting a tail, he should have spotted someone following him for that long.

He ran through a quick mental log of his activities over the past seven days. Her mastery of disguises was very impressive, and he needed to find out if she might have stumbled onto anything that would jeopardize his investigation. He didn't think so, but he'd have to be sure.

The city landscape dwindled and changed. Elf/Angel settled a little deeper into her seat and accelerated. The speedometer crept higher, leaving sixty behind and pushing seventy. He waited for the car to protest the speed with various vibrations and rattles. Instead, the engine purred like a very contented cat.

"You still haven't told me where you're taking me."

"It's Friday afternoon. We're going where all the good Minnesotans go on a summer weekend."

"I'm not from around here. Enlighten me."

"On the weekend, everyone goes up north to the cabin on the lake. We're going up north."

"That I can see. Where up north?"

"To the lake."

"The lake. According to your license plate, there's more than one."

"True. But the only one that counts is the one we're going to."

"And that would be…?"

"The one where the cabin is." She smiled and her dimple winked at him. "You're kind of slow, aren't you?"

"You're killing me, Elf."

She chuckled, and the husky sound sent images of late-night intimacies flashing through his mind. He shifted, trying to get more comfortable. Between tight legroom and tightening pants, it wasn't easy.

"Any chance you'll be stopping for gas? Soon?"

"Just filled the tank before I picked you up, so no, I'm not planning on it. I'd like to get mostly there before full dark."

He muttered a soft curse and shifted again, still finding no comfort.

Elf gave him a quick once-over, a frown creasing her forehead. "Something wrong?"

"Nothing access to a rest room wouldn't solve."

"Ah." The frown deepened. "Hmm."

"I take it you hadn't considered the need for rest stops before you hustled me out of that room?"

"No."

"Understandable. You can't be expected to think of everything."

Red crept up her neck and stained her cheeks. Interesting. Was she embarrassed by the situation or mad at not having thought of the eventuality?

"Of course, it wouldn't be so bad if you hadn't forced that glass of doctored water down my throat." He twisted the guilt knot a little tighter.

The flush deepened. "Sedatives are a workable, short-term convenience."

Short-term. She hadn't planned on keeping him in custody for very long. Another interesting detail. "Your planning skills could use a little work." He waved his free hand. "Never mind, I'll manage."

They were approaching an exit ramp. Elf flipped on her turn signal. The ramp led to a rest stop where a steady procession of cars and trucks pulling campers and boats performed the weekend drivers' ballet.

If he could get away from her, it would be easy enough to catch a ride out of there.

She maneuvered into an empty parking spot some distance from the main building. The car keys jingled in the silence when she pulled them out of the ignition and dropped them into a lower pant-leg pocket. "You're left-handed, right?"

"Yeah. Why?"

"Just working out the logistics." She stretched between the bucket seats and grabbed something from the back seat before getting out.

Her vanilla fragrance still floated in the air. If it hadn't been for that scent, he wouldn't have made the connection between Elf's disguises nearly so fast; the change in her appearance had been so complete.

She stretched, giving him an unexpected glimpse of her bared midriff. Was that...? She rounded the car to the passenger door and pulled it open. He got another glimpse, just before she hunkered down beside him. It was. She had a pierced navel. And a pierced nose. He wondered what other parts of her body sported nontraditional jewelry.

A handcuff closing around his right wrist broke into his ponderings. She reached over and freed his left hand, then stood, tugging him out of his seat. Her left hand, warm and slightly callused, held his right hand, and he realized she'd cuffed them together. The dark blue sweatshirt she'd pulled out of the back seat draped casually over her wrist, hiding the cuffs.

Interesting. He couldn't wait to see what she had planned next.

The rest stop consisted of one main building and a couple of smaller structures spread across a wide, grassy expanse. She led him on a meandering path towards one of the outbuildings, which sported a Family Rest Room sign. A mother with two small boys exited the structure and Elf tugged him in, locking the door behind them.

He gave the facility a quick scan, then turned to her. She was studying the cinderblock construction of the rest room, too. "Elf?"

She shrugged. "This is the best I can manage until we get to the lake. You better not have a bashful bladder, because that window's too low, too large and on the wrong side of the building for me to cover both exits."

Figures she'd notice the same things he had. "You expect me to—" He looked around the large, *open* room. Sink, towel dispenser, wastepaper can, diaper-changing table…. No stall door. No stall. Everything was out in plain view. "This is a joke, right?"

She shook her head and glared at him. "And I'm not taking the cuffs off, so don't even bother to ask."

"You know, this just isn't right, on so many levels, I can't begin—"

"Then don't bother. Or do, but do it while you're…" She gestured towards the urinal.

He shook his head and crossed the room, with her a

half step behind him. He began undoing the button fly of his Levi's. Her arm moved in unison with his. She pulled the sweatshirt off their wrists and stood beside him, staring straight ahead.

"Uh, Elf?"

"What."

"About those logistics you were working out?"

"Yeah, what?"

"I am left-handed, but for some things, I need to use my right hand."

She looked at him out of the corner of her eyes as they widened with realization. "You're kidding."

"Trust me, I'm not."

She looked around the room. A tiny groan and a hang of her head told him she noticed the same problem he had—no exposed pipes she could cuff him to while he took care of business.

By his best reckoning, there were two options. Either they stayed cuffed together, or she let him loose.

Without cuffs on, he could use the advantages of his height and strength. Would she take that risk?

Or had she been at this job so long, she wouldn't mind dealing with a little intimacy usually reserved for couples not held together by stainless steel bracelets?

She tilted her head from side to side, like she was trying to ease tight muscles, and heaved a deep sigh. "All right, already. Get on with it."

"Yes, ma'am." He let loose with a big sigh of his own.

This would go down in agency history as one of the oddest situations ever. Not that he'd tell anyone about it. He'd never live down the jokes.

Chapter 3

Angel got Cabrini back in the car without incident. Traffic was light and no highway patrols were in evidence. After the bathroom incident, the rest of the trip up north seemed downright boring.

The uneventful drive gave her plenty of time to mull over the current situation and her reactions to her passenger. They were going to be in close confines for the next couple days.

She needed to get a grip... The image of them standing side by side in the rest room floated by her mind's eye, triggering a warm shiver.

If she didn't get her thoughts under control, she wouldn't have to worry about the weekend, because she'd never last the first night.

Focus on Dex's woodland retreat. That should be a safe topic, and it held the biggest concern.

"Cabin" really was a misnomer for the place. It called up images of seclusion and rustic living. The most rustic aspect of Dex's place was the lack of a phone. Otherwise, with three bedrooms, two baths, a whirlpool tub and indoor sauna, his cabin was better fixtured than many homes. It seemed like such a waste, out in the middle of nowhere.

· Even so, with all those amenities, there wasn't much available to keep a reluctant guest in place. She would have to rely on the remote location to dissuade Cabrini from trying to run anywhere.

For his part, Cabrini held his own counsel. He seemed much more interested in tracking their progress as the towns became smaller and the birch and pine woods closed in on the two-lane road. He made no effort to initiate any kind of conversation with her, which suited her just fine.

She made good time to the secluded tract of land, located on one of the many lakes that Swiss-cheesed the northern Minnesota landscape.

Twilight settled as she left the secondary road to take the narrow, gravel lane leading to Dex's cabin. By the time she reached their final destination, full dark lay beneath the tall pines.

Inky shadows surrounded and filled the small clearing. The sky overhead resembled a swath of black velvet with diamonds randomly strewn across it. The new moon provided little light.

She swung the car around the curved drive in front of the cabin, stopping when her headlights shone on the door.

"Hang tight for a second. I'll get the door open and some lights on."

"Don't worry about me, Elf." Cabrini rattled the handcuffs holding him to his seat. "I promise not to wander off too far without you."

Her jaw tightened. Ever since he'd realized she didn't

like the situation, he seemed to take great delight in reminding her how close she skated to legal lines.

Had her client been anyone other than Dex, she would have walked away from the assignment at the first hint of illegality. The car door rattled as she slammed it shut.

The summer warmth had cooled slightly with the sunset. She pulled on her navy blue zip-front sweatshirt before she grabbed one of the bags of groceries from the trunk and climbed the steps to the full-length front porch.

The same jiggle of the key she remembered got the lock open. The screen door sighed shut behind her. She left the solid wood interior door standing wide as she walked farther into the room, finding light switches from memory. By the time she deposited the grocery bag in the open, spacious kitchen, the first floor blazed with lights.

Angel made another quick trip to haul in their clothes and the rest of her supplies, but took her time returning to get Cabrini. The whole situation of having him in custody and bringing him here created a logistical nightmare.

Under normal circumstances, when she took a bail jumper into custody, she turned the perp over to the closest law enforcement agency at the first available opportunity.

She'd never taken one away for the weekend. Dex better have a very good reason for putting her in this position.

What was she going to do with Cabrini? That he hadn't resisted in any way didn't mean he wouldn't at some point in the future.

She couldn't keep drugging him, not for the whole weekend. The very idea churned her stomach.

Locking him up somewhere wasn't viable. There was no place to tie him up, either. Her stomach did another grind.

She never should have agreed to Dex's request. Especially when he wouldn't give her all the details. There were just too many variables, and none of them felt particularly comfortable. Especially the fact that Cabrini seemed to be guilty of nothing more than sticking his nose where it didn't belong.

She jammed her fists into her pockets. Something sharp jabbed her hand. She pulled the envelope containing Dex's note from her pocket and ripped it open. The typed message was short and to the point.

New arson cases have prompted a reopening of our old arson files. Cabrini is a central figure and must be kept sequestered at this time. You'll appreciate the need to keep details confidential for a while longer.

Well, that helped. But not much.

Her cell phone played the first notes of "The Hokey Pokey." The screen displayed a familiar number, along with the symbol showing limited reception.

"Hello, Dex."

"Are you someplace you can talk?"

"We just got to your cabin."

"You made it okay? No…incidents?"

The image of standing next to Cabrini as he relieved himself, her hand in far too near a proximity to his bare flesh, flashed through her mind. "Incidents? No. Everything went…fine."

"Where is Cabrini?"

"He's still in the car. I haven't quite worked out how I'm going to keep him contained until we head back."

"I'm sure you'll come up with something."

Easy for him to say. Angel began pacing back and forth in the foyer, glancing out at the car each time she passed the open door. Dex wasn't facing forty-eight hours of close contact with a dangerously attractive stranger.

"Did you get…I left…the key?" His voice cut in and out as the reception weakened.

"Yes." Her hand clenched around the cell phone and she stood still. "You didn't give me very much to go on."

"The investigation…my attention. Potential for blackmail…"

"What? Dex, repeat. I'm losing the signal."

"Cabrini…your father. I need you to…"

"Dex? You need me to what?"

"…hear you. Trust… You'll underst—"

The line went dead. Angel pulled the phone from her ear and glared at the display screen now showing the no service symbol. Modern technology sucked when it didn't work.

She homed in on what portion of Dex's conversation she had been able to hear. Arson, blackmail, Cabrini, her father. How did they fit together?

She ran her free hand through her hair, giving her scalp a good scratching. Related to Dad's murder? The odds seemed awfully high against that possibility. Related how?

Someday, please God, let it be, she would track down the person responsible. Then, maybe, her mother could recover and they could find some peace.

Was it possible she was closer to that day than she realized? How did Cabrini tie into all this?

She paced back and forth, trying to get the pieces of the puzzle to fit, but there was just too little to work with. On one level she found it flattering that Dex had asked for her help. It was an indication of his trust. On another level it angered her that he hadn't trusted her enough to tell her everything.

If he wasn't family... She stopped the thought. He was the closest thing she'd had to a father since she was ten years old. He trusted her enough to ask for her help. She should trust him enough to believe he wouldn't endanger her livelihood. Or her life.

She just wished she had her real father to turn to for advice.

Frank watched Elf pace back and forth behind the screen door. Whoever she was talking to wasn't making her happy. Maybe it was her client.

Who was her client and what kind of hold did he have on her? She clearly hadn't liked using drugs as a means of control, yet she had taken that risk to accomplish her assignment.

Loyalty and determination were strong motivators. In his field, those traits could mean the difference between success and failure, life and death.

She flipped the phone closed and stowed it in one of her many pants pockets. He expected her to come get him, but instead, she stood with her fists braced on her hips, staring down at the ground.

He could almost feel sorry for her. With her short, spiky hair and current costume, she almost looked waif-like. Of course, waifs didn't normally pack snub-nosed revolvers.

She began pacing again. Something bothered her, which was only fair considering she'd been bothering him since the first glimpse he'd caught of her.

It wasn't every day a woman got the better of him.

He'd tasted sweet revenge, brief as it was, back at the rest stop. That satisfaction had come with a price and he'd paid with a constant state of discomfort, aggravated every time his traitorous memory opted to review the image of her hand so close to his. Which seemed to happen with every mile marker they had passed in silence on their long drive to the middle of nowhere.

She'd given no indication of how long they would be staying here. He'd lay odds they wouldn't leave until her client instructed her to do so.

Her client's identity would be an extremely helpful detail to know right about now.

Someone had broken his cover. He wanted to know who and why. And he wanted to know how and why this woman was involved.

Elf looked up and met his gaze head-on. He could see her take a deep breath before she headed back to the car with a determined step.

"Okay, Cabrini, here's the deal." She pulled the passenger door open, but made no move to release him. "We're going to be here for a couple days. Maybe longer. While this place is fully equipped, it does lack anything that resembles a jail cell."

"I can see where that might pose a problem."

"Especially for you. I don't have a secure place to keep you, and my options seem pretty limited."

"Exhausted your supply of knockout drugs, did you?" How much did she dislike holding him against his will?

In the dim light from the car dome fixture, her deep blue irises looked black. He could almost hear the crackle of anger in her eyes.

Quite a bit, it would seem. "No iron bed to handcuff me to?"

A muscle in her jaw pulsed as she ground her teeth.

"No woodshed, root cellar or pool house?" He pushed a little more.

She slapped the roof of the car as she straightened away from the door. "Having fun, aren't you?"

"Surprisingly, yes." He winked at her.

She stomped away a few steps, spun around and jammed her fists into her pockets. "Okay. Fine. Now that you've enumerated what we don't have, would you like to make any suggestions about what would work?"

"You could just ask me."

"Ask you what?"

"To cooperate."

"Of course." She smacked her forehead. "Why didn't I think of that? The clientele I deal with is always cooperative and trustworthy."

"I thought we established that I'm not your usual kind of target."

She crossed back to the car, rested her hands on the roof and leaned down to look him in the eyes. "Mistah Cabrini, suh?"

Oh, hell. Southern.

"Would you all be so kind as to behave yourself while we're all alone out here in the middle of nowhere?" She batted her long, black eyelashes at him.

"Sure."

"Yeah. Right." She pushed away from the car again but didn't move.

That put him eye to belly button with her again. The tiny red crystal beads dangling from the gold ring piercing her navel winked at him, teasing him with intimate images. His fingers itched to slip under her clothes and explore her vanilla-scented skin.

He cleared his throat. "You could try trusting me."

"Why would I do that?"

"We've established there's no legal grounds for you to hold me." He shrugged. "Have I done anything to make you distrust me?"

"No. But then, you've been restrained most of the time."

"True enough. How about this? How much do you trust your client?"

"What do you mean?"

"Would he ask you to kidnap someone and take them out of town if he thought that person was dangerous?"

"That may be *exactly* why he asked me to bring you here. I do this for a living. He knew I'd be safe and that he could trust me."

"Is that what he just told you?"

Her hand brushed across the pocket holding her phone. "The signal kept breaking up. I couldn't make out everything he said."

"How much did you hear?"

"Enough to know you're in the middle of something."

"That's a lot of help. Any idea what?"

She studied him through narrowed eyes. "What do you know about arson?"

His heart skipped sideways for a beat. Did she know about his investigation, or was she fishing for information? "Enough to know it's not a good idea."

"Blackmail?"

He shook his head. His agency's client hadn't mentioned blackmail, but he wouldn't be surprised if it did crop up somewhere during his investigation. "Same thing. All around bad idea."

"Who are you, really? What do you do?"

"You've been following me for a week. Why don't you tell me?" He wanted to hear how much she'd learned while shadowing him.

"You live simply, which is probably a good thing since you have no visible means of support and you don't seem to be in any hurry to find a job. You don't seem to have a circle of friends, either, so you're prob-

ably new in town. You don't eat out much and seldom
have more than one beer. More often than not, when you
went to the bar you drank straight tonic water. With a
twist of lime." She paused, then added, "And you like
clothes that fit well."

"That's it?" It might sound like an impressive list, but
there was nothing in her recitation to indicate she had
stumbled onto anything of significance.

"You drive a Taurus, which seems a bit odd." She
gave him a once-over. "But, the tags are going to ex-
pire in a few months. So you may have picked it up
cheap at a police auction or something. More often than
not, you take the bus to the library, where you spend a
lot of time. What are you researching?"

Scratch the part about nothing significant. "You're
sure it's research?"

"It's not porn sites and it's not day-trading. Mostly
you've been visiting newspaper archives, with old property records and court reports thrown in for variety."

"I like to get to know a city when I arrive." He
shrugged it off, pretending it held little importance.

She shook her head. "Maybe, but my instincts tell me
there's a lot more beneath the surface."

Her instincts were good. Damn.

His investigation was still intact—there was no way
for her to pinpoint exactly what he was digging into—
but she knew more than he'd expected.

His best course would be to control how much more
she uncovered. With a little luck and a lot of skill, he
could lead her where he needed to go.

"Gut reactions can be pretty reliable. Maybe you
should trust yours."

"Why?"

"You mentioned arson. I'm digging into some cold
cases that have been ignored for too long."

She squatted beside him, bracing her hands on either side of the door frame, and stared at him with rounded eyes. "What?"

That surprised her. Good. "You're interfering with an ongoing investigation."

She stood in a rush and stumbled back a few steps. "Where are you from?"

"Washington, D.C." Let's see where that leads her.

"FBI?" She took another step back. "ATF?"

He didn't want to outright lie to her, so he tilted his head and let her draw her own conclusions for now.

"Aw, sh—boygan!" She began pacing.

"Sheboygan?"

"My mother doesn't like it when I swear."

"Sheboygan?" he repeated. "You're a bounty hunter and you don't swear?"

"Profanity shows a lack of imagination."

"The folks in Sheboygan probably wouldn't appreciate having their town taken in vain."

"They can get in line with the folks from Keister."

He laughed.

He sat there, north of who knew where, handcuffed to the seat of a rusting shell that hid a high-performance engine. A two-month investigation was in jeopardy. He'd just manipulated the assumptions of his captor, a woman who had drugged him and held him at gunpoint—and managed to look too damn sexy doing it, even punked out like she was.

And she made him laugh.

Laughing felt good. It had been a long time since he'd laughed. "Come on, Elf. Trust me. What have you got to lose?"

"Only my self-respect." She kept pacing, kicking at the gravel drive. "I don't suppose you can prove who you are? No official ID or anything like that?"

"What kind of undercover agent would I be if I carried proof of my real identity on me? Before you ask—" he held up his free hand when she opened her mouth "—you won't find proof in my room, either."

"Any suggestions on how I can verify who you say you are?"

"Unfortunately, it's Friday night and even my boss, workaholic that she is, leaves the office for the weekend." No need to let on that his boss was always reachable—not yet, anyway.

"Convenient."

"True, nonetheless. We could try calling her. She might have her line forwarded."

"No phone in the cabin and the cell phone is intermittent, as I just learned. This doesn't make sense. Why would Dex—" She interrupted herself. "This is crazy."

Dex? Her client? "It's up to you, Elf."

"What guarantee do I have that you won't rabbit the second I turn my back?"

"None. Except my word."

"Oh, that's real reassuring."

"Look. I'm from the east coast. I've never been to Minnesota before this assignment. I have no clue where we are, where the closest town might be or if there even is a town within hiking distance. All I know is that we're near a lake and the mosquitoes—" he smacked a specimen trying to suck his neck dry "—are hungry little buggers. Could we at least go inside?"

She stopped pacing and approached the car. "You're keeping the cuffs on, at least until I figure out…something."

"You're the boss."

Her *Yeah, right* sideways glance at him made it clear just what she thought of that statement's credibility. "Sit on your right hand."

He obeyed, sliding his free hand under his leg. She pinned his leg in place with her knee, putting more weight than necessary on it, as she leaned into the car and released the handcuff from the seat frame. Her warm scent surrounded him, filling his head with all sorts of imaginings better left for late nights and soft beds.

She backed out of the car, but kept a firm hold on his handcuffed wrist. "Let's see if we can do this nice and easy. Swing your legs out of the car, stand up and turn around."

He followed her directions, hesitating for a couple heartbeats when he stood at his full height. She was close. Close enough he could feel her warm breath fanning the exposed skin of his throat.

Close enough he could see her swallow and watch the dawning awareness in her eyes.

Close enough she'd notice exactly how…aware he was in a couple seconds. He turned his back to her.

A soft breeze brushed the back of his neck.

Or maybe it was her sighed release of a held breath.

Blood heated low in his belly. If he didn't watch out, this attraction would get out of hand way too easily. He'd already broken one of his rules by talking to a civilian about his assignment. He stood dangerously close to breaking a few more.

Angel snapped the handcuff into place around Cabrini's right wrist. Beneath her fingers, his pulse beat with a heavy rhythm that matched her own heartbeat. She forced out a calming breath and, along with it, the memory of the hungry desire she'd read in his eyes.

Was he really a federal agent? If he was telling the truth, what the devil was Dex up to and why had he involved her?

Anger bubbled up and she embraced the emotion. Anything was better than the desire Cabrini's proximity generated.

Another mosquito landed on Cabrini's neck and she slapped it, maybe a little harder than necessary, judging by his startled glance over his shoulder at her.

"The bugs seem to have a particular liking for your taste." Sweet or salty? The thought sent heat flashing over her neck and cheeks. She kicked Rusty's door shut and nudged Cabrini in the direction of the house. "Let's get inside before they make a meal of you."

Once inside, she shut and locked the inner door and turned off the porch light. She tapped Cabrini's shoulder and nodded toward the breakfast nook. "Have a seat."

He folded his length onto the bench and slid into the corner. It gave him a power position from which he could observe her, but it also severely restricted his mobility. If he made any unexpected move, she'd have her gun out and at the ready before he could do more than slide to the end of the table.

"Thanks." She acknowledged his tactic.

"I figure the only way to earn your trust is to behave in a trustworthy manner."

"Let's really put you to the test then."

He sat up a little straighter. "What do you have in mind?"

"Cooking." She shrugged at his raised eyebrows. "I'm not very good and have a rather limited repertoire. Tonight's options are mac and cheese or tomato soup and grilled cheese sandwiches."

"Kind of heavy on the cheese, aren't you?"

"Just doing my part to support the local economy." She began unpacking the grocery bag. "Pick your poison—which will it be?"

"I'll leave it to you."

"Macaroni and cheese it is." She put water on to boil. "It's more of a one-handed meal, which is all you'll have available after I cuff you to the table leg."

It only took a few minutes to stow the rest of the groceries in the cupboard, then she set about readying the ingredients for their meal. All the while, she was acutely aware of his steady gaze on her as she moved around the kitchen work island dicing ham and cheese.

"No box?" His question caught her by surprise.

"Nope. Scratch." She tossed the cheese and ham into the pot with the drained pasta, added some milk and stirred.

"Isn't a box easier?"

"Not really, and this tastes a whole lot better." Satisfied with the progress of their meal preparation, she turned her attention to the next item on her agenda—securing Cabrini while they ate. "Which hand do you eat with?"

The wicked twinkle in his eyes told her he was remembering the rest stop and her logistical error. A slow smile curved his lips. An answering heat crept up her neck.

Manitoba. She hadn't blushed this much since... ever.

She had a bad feeling she better get used to the heat.

Chapter 4

Frank lounged back against the cushioned kitchen banquette. In spite of her warning, the meal had been rather tasty, if heavy on the dairy products and lacking in the vegetable food group.

The handcuffs rattled as he stretched his arms and rolled his shoulders. His dining posture left something to be desired. The table leg she'd cuffed him to was positioned too far under the table for him to sit upright.

He rattled the cuffs again, drawing her attention. "Could I interest you in undoing these?"

"Why would I do that?" Eating hadn't noticeably improved her disposition.

"It'll be easier for me to do the dishes without the bracelets."

"You want to do the dishes?"

"I've never known anyone who *wants* to clean dishes. It just seems a fair offer to make since you did the cooking. It was quite good, by the way. I don't think I've had macaroni and cheese since I was twelve."

"Hmph."

"Figure out your problem yet?" They'd eaten their meal in silence. Neither of them had offered any conversation openers. He'd spent the time mulling over the situation and trying to come up with a plan.

"What problem?"

"Whatever it is that's been eating at you for the past half hour."

"The problem part is easy. It's the solution that has me stumped."

"Let me guess. I'm your problem?"

"Perceptive, aren't you?"

"Still haven't decided if you believe me?"

"Whether or not I do, I'm still stuck." She dropped her head into her hands and dug her fingers into her hair. "Which agency did you say you work for?"

"Tell you what. Why don't you take the cuffs off and I'll answer all your questions while I deal with the dishes."

She didn't answer.

"Consider it a test."

She blew out a breath and pushed away from the table. "You'll answer all my questions?"

"All that I can without jeopardizing my investigation."

She snorted. "That's convenient. Anything I ask that you don't want to answer, you just claim classified, is that it?"

"Even if it is, you'll still get the dishes washed and the kitchen cleaned up. That must be worth something."

"Fine. Turn around."

He complied, twisting his right arm behind him as he faced the wall. She was still plenty wary and not tak-

ing any chances. Every time she uncuffed him, she
made sure he was in as awkward a position as she could
come up with.

The cuff loosened and he waited for her next direction. He really wanted to win her trust, and figured it
would be in his best interest to comply with her requests
and not move until so ordered.

"Stand up."

He turned slowly and found her standing across the
table from him with her gun drawn. Laying both hands
on the table, he slid to the end of the seat and stood.

"I didn't find any soap for the dishwasher, so you'll
have to do this the old-fashioned way. There's dish soap
in the cabinet under the sink."

He nodded, gathered up the dishes and moved to the
sink. The black of night beyond the glass turned the
window over the sink into a mirror. He could watch her
as he worked with his back to her. Water splashed, suds
grew and silence fell.

"No questions?" he prompted.

She stood behind him, her arms crossed, her gun
resting at the ready. "Who did you say you work for?"

Time for a little more trust-building. "Actually, I
never said."

"You aren't really a Fed, are you?" An undercurrent
of anger shaded her words.

"No."

He heard something that sounded suspiciously like
"Sanibel." Was she more pissed off that he hadn't told
her the truth or that she'd jumped to the wrong conclusion? "If it makes you feel any better, I was with the
ATF up until about a year ago."

"What happened?"

"Nothing." Nothing he'd talk about. "Just time for a
change."

"Are you freelance or part of an agency?"

"The Diamond Group is a moderate-sized, highly respected private investigation firm in Washington D.C."

"Isn't that nice. What's it got to do with you?"

No more assumptions on her part. He smiled. She learned quick. "I'm on the staff."

"So, what are you doing in Minneapolis?"

"We've been contracted to look into an old case that never closed."

"Who hired you?"

He shook his head. "There we're getting into client confidentiality. You can appreciate that, I'm sure."

The distortions of the window didn't lessen the impact of her glare at him. He waited for her next question.

"If you can't tell me who your client is, will you tell me what you're investigating?"

"Arson."

She straightened and their eyes met in the dark glass.

"I don't suppose you can tell me what you've learned."

"Sorry, Elf. I'm a long ways from writing the final report. Especially with this unexpected interruption in my schedule."

Her sigh told him his little dig had landed on target. He wiped his hands and draped the dish towel over the dishes in the drainer. When he turned around, he caught her in midyawn.

"Tired?" He glanced at the clock on the wall then double-checked the time with his watch. It was nearly one in the morning. "Strange. It's late, but I'm not that tired. In fact, I'm feeling rather well-rested."

She scowled at him. "We're back to my problem. How am I going to secure you for the night?"

"Do you suppose the owner of this place is into bondage? Maybe he has an extra set of cuffs…."

Elf turned a furious red from her collarbone to her scalp. He grinned. "Guess not, huh?"

"I would find it highly unlikely."

"So this place isn't yours? Who does own it?"

"My…uncle." Her slight hesitation didn't escape his notice. "He was good enough to let me borrow the cabin for the weekend."

"Cabin?" He looked around at the butcher-block counters and stainless steel appliances. The kitchen was as well-equipped as his back home. If the rest of the house was as modern, it would fit right into some of the newer housing developments he'd seen around the Twin Cities area.

"Oh, don't even go there. It's ostentatious and ridiculous, I know. He never had a family of his own to spend his money on, so it all went to…stuff. I wish he could have found better use—" Her mouth snapped shut with a sharp click of teeth. "Turn around."

She had him cuffed and moving towards the stairs before he could figure out what her outburst might mean. He tucked the information away for later.

Upstairs, the bedrooms carried through on the promise of the first floor. Decorated in what some designer probably considered rustic charm, the rooms reminded him of a bed-and-breakfast he'd stayed in once. He'd intended for that weekend outing to end with a romantic proposal. Then he'd discovered the truth about his almost-fiancée's "love." He shied away from any more memories of the disaster he'd barely avoided.

They stopped just inside the door of the second bedroom. It was the smallest and farthest from the top of the stairs. Colorful rag rugs warmed the hardwood floor. The bed was a roomy queen with a Shaker-style headboard.

"Good. I hoped this bed was still here." She nudged

him into the room. "This will work just fine." The gym bag she'd carried up landed on top of the blanket chest at the foot of the bed.

"You're pretty familiar with the place."

"We used to come up here during the summer when I was little, but I haven't been since high school." She motioned him farther into the room. "I wasn't sure how much of the furniture I remembered would still be here."

"You and your uncle?"

"And Mom." A sad tone entered her voice. Another bit of information for future consideration.

She zipped open the bag and pulled out a few items. "The bathroom." She nodded toward the door and followed him into the short hall.

The two smaller bedrooms shared a bathroom with a single entrance from the hallway. She turned on the light and stepped aside for him to enter. As she unlocked the cuffs, his quick recon of the room revealed pretty much what he'd expected. No second door and no window big enough for him to squeeze through to freedom.

He turned to face her and she pushed the small pile of items into his hands. "Five minutes. Plenty of time for you to come up with some sort of weapon. Unless you're serious about wanting me to trust you." She stepped back and pulled the door closed.

He set the soap, toothbrush and toothpaste, all still in their wrappers, on the counter and shook out the last item.

"Hey, Elf. What are the shorts for?"

"To sleep in."

"I don't normally—"

"This isn't normal. This is Minnesota and you'll sleep in shorts."

"Testy, testy." He smothered a chuckle and silently

thanked her for the foresight. Sleeping in the nude might be his preference, but he didn't care for that sort of exposure in this sort of situation.

Between his boxers and the shorts, he might stand a chance of disguising the evidence of his body's intense reaction to her every time she got close to him.

Three minutes later, two minutes before she intended to pound on the door and roust him, the bathroom door swung open to reveal a half-naked Frank Cabrini.

Angel's breath caught in her throat. *Helsinki. He's gorgeous.* Broad shoulders, defined muscles, golden tan. A light dusting of coal-black hair covered his chest, narrowing over his six-pack abs and disappearing into the waistband of the navy knit shorts she'd picked up as an afterthought.

She kind of regretted having had that afterthought.

Insane or dead. She was going to be one or the other before the weekend was over.

"Keep looking at me like that and I won't be held responsible for the results." He reached out and tapped her chin, confirming her fear that her mouth had fallen open. "Do you want to search me, in case I did come up with a weapon?"

She didn't want to but couldn't stop from dropping her gaze to the front of his shorts. A wave of heat started somewhere in the vicinity of her chest, flowing up in embarrassment and rolling down in hunger.

She stepped back. "Uh, right." A slow, deep breath got her brain functioning. "That's not necessary." She took another step back and gestured towards the bedroom. Everything she could think of to say was fraught with innuendo.

He led the way into the guest room. His rear view was as delightful as the front. She trailed after him, keeping a safe distance.

"Okay, then. I know your wrists are probably getting kind of sore, so I dug out the first-aid kit. We can use the gauze for a little protection."

"Did you think of that before or after you wrapped the headboard?"

"About the same time, actually." She'd wrapped two slats, one on either side of the headboard. "I noticed some scratches on the table leg, and I'd like to keep the damage—to you and the furniture—to a minimum."

"You're a peach, Elf." He sat on the edge of the bed and bounced a little, testing the mattress' firmness.

Those blasted eyes of his held her captive, looking into her soul again. She glanced away and picked up the roll of gauze. "Any preference which wrist?"

"Either will be fine."

"Your right, I think." She waited for him to hold out his arm before she approached him. It took an eternity of seconds to wind a few strips of bandage around his wrist. She kept talking, partly to distract herself from the heat of his skin beneath her fingers and partly to explain herself. "I'm sure that, given enough time, you could find a way to get out of the cuffs."

"Then why bother with them?"

"The illusion." She risked a quick glance at his face. "You want me to trust you. I can't, not without proof."

"Isn't trust believing without proof?"

She considered that for a moment. "I suppose it is. However you want to define trust, I'm a long ways away from it when it comes to you."

The handcuffs rattled as she picked them up from the bedside stand. "Consider this another test."

"What do I get if I pass?"

"I'll trust you as long as I'm awake and can see you."

"That doesn't sound much like trust to me."

She shrugged. "It's the best I can offer. Lie down."

He stretched out on the bed and lifted his right arm over his head, holding it in place against the wrapped slat, waiting for her to shackle him to the bed.

Her mouth went dry. She'd miscalculated and would have to get too close to him. The metal of the cuffs bit into her hand as she clenched her fist. She could take the coward's route and have him do it himself, but she'd still have to get close to make sure both cuffs were fully engaged.

And she wasn't a coward. She knelt on the bed and attached the first cuff to his wrist.

The muscles in his arm flexed. She understood the involuntary reaction. She'd responded the same way the few times she'd been cuffed.

The metal ratcheted closed around the headboard slat. Before she could move away and take a relieved breath, she found her own wrist held fast in Frank's free hand.

He pulled her off balance and she landed across his chest. Her breath escaped in a startled gasp as he rolled. Faster than she could react, he had her half-pinned in place with her arm behind her back and his leg thrown over hers.

She went utterly still, berating herself for being so careless and getting caught off guard. Neither of them moved for the span of a few heartbeats.

Then he lowered his head and brushed her lips with his in the softest of kisses, over almost before it had begun.

She held her breath, startled at the gentle touch, afraid he'd kiss her again, afraid he wouldn't.

He dipped his head and kissed her again, just a fleeting touch.

She licked her lips, wanting to capture the taste of him on her tongue, and felt cheated when she found no trace.

Again he returned, nibbling at her lips in a delicate combination that coaxed them open and allowed him access that he declined.

Instead, he trailed a path across her cheek to her jaw and down her throat. Heat followed.

Her world tilted out of alignment as awareness and hunger flashed to life.

Frank rolled again, this time pulling her on top of him. From chest to knees, they touched. There was no denying his reaction to her.

He took a deep breath and let it out on a slow sigh. "We may not trust each other, but make no mistake. Before we go our separate ways, we're going to find ourselves in this same position, sans clothes and handcuffs. We will finish this, Elf."

He released her arm and slid his hand beneath his head, pinning it there, no longer touching her.

The instant she realized she was free, she scrambled off him and backed to the door. "That would be a big mistake."

"Probably." He held her in place with a look, palpable as a caress, that devoured every detail of her appearance. "But it will happen."

"No, it won't." She slapped the light switch, sending the room into welcome darkness. "We can't."

The door closed behind her, blocking him from sight, but not memory. She went into the bathroom, needing to put another barrier, and more space, between them.

The bathroom door latched with a soft click. She slid down the cool wood to sit on the cooler tile floor, hoping to chill the heat throbbing through her body.

Stupid, stupid, stupid. She'd gotten careless on so many levels she could hardly begin to sort out everything.

It all started with Dex. She should never have taken him on as a client.

Shouldn't have started the case without a clear understanding of the timeline.

Should never have taken Cabrini into custody without a legal warrant.

The "shouldn'ts" piled up, each mistake on top of the last one, until Cabrini had landed on top of her on a bed.

She'd let him kiss her, had kissed him back. Would have let it go further without a thought of the consequences.

She was certifiable.

She'd escaped intact, this time. She couldn't afford to let there be a next time.

Chapter 5

The eerie call of a loon beckoned the morning sun. Mist hung over the lake, a living example of the smoky waters Minnesota had been named for. Angel sat on the edge of the dock, absorbing the fresh air, peace and beauty surrounding her.

On one level, she loved the solitude. She appreciated the momentary escape from her life in the city. On another level, she was going crazy sitting here. She needed to be doing something productive, not sitting and waiting for Dex's next call.

She'd already heard about the possible link between some old arson cases, including the one resulting in her father's death, and the new rash of fires. George McDonough, her contact on the squad, had noticed the similarities and alerted her.

What she didn't know was how Dex had come to connect Cabrini to the cases. If she could discover his client's identity, she might be able to piece it all together.

The questions had her itching to do some investigating of her own.

She pushed to her feet and paced the length of the rough wood dock. Every spare minute she could squeeze out of her life, she devoted to her own investigation. Over the years, she'd built up a considerable file of dead ends, shadows and smoke. Even so, each new lead teased her with the possibility of solving the case. She needed to find the killer. For her mother and for herself.

Another loon call broke over the lake. The haunting tones faded into the surrounding pine forest. It was still early, but she'd better check on her "guest," see if he needed anything.

Her feet dragged at the thought of facing him after last night. Their kiss still warmed her lips every time she allowed the memory to slip into her awareness.

What had possessed her?

Silly question. Cabrini and his fallen-altar-boy looks, smoldering eyes and body to die for, that's what had possessed her.

She played with the thought of instigating a repeat performance, but sent the idea running with a simple reminder.

At the moment, they weren't exactly on the same side. She had a job. He *was* the job. And the job did not involve swapping bodily fluids. No matter how curious she might be about the whole possibility.

She slid the patio door shut behind her and padded upstairs. Her bare feet made little noise. If Cabrini was up to something, she'd catch him at it. She eased the bedroom door open and found him sitting on the neatly made bed, his perfect lotus position only slightly marred by the handcuffs still holding his right hand against the headboard.

Meditation. Who'da thought it? She began to close the door.

"Good morning." His voice sounded relaxed and refreshed. His eyes were still closed and he looked relaxed and refreshed. But then he should—he'd had enough sleep in the last twenty-four hours.

She, on the other hand, had had almost no sleep. She felt like leftover pasta—lumpy, sticky and stiff. "Don't let me interrupt."

"Just finished." He opened his eyes. "Holy Hanna, Elf. You look like hell."

"Gee, thanks. Just what a girl likes to hear first thing in the morning."

He ignored her sarcasm. "Did you get any sleep?"

"Enough." That conversation would get old fast. She changed the subject. "I'm going to take a shower. Would you like to make use of the bathroom first?"

"Sure. Then I can get breakfast started while you're in there."

"Nice offer, but I'm not buying it."

He shrugged. "It was worth a try, though, don't you think?" He gave a lopsided grin, his white teeth a startling contrast to his black beard.

"As if." She donned Valley Girl to distract him while she unlocked the cuffs. "You are, like, so totally busted."

He reached for her and she took a quick step back. Memory of how easily he'd pulled her under him last night sent her pulse into overdrive.

Judging by his physical response to her nearness, he remembered, too.

No repeats.

She motioned to the door with her gun and followed at a safe distance.

* * *

"Did I pass the test?" Frank wedged himself back onto the breakfast nook bench.

"Oh, yeah. Flying colors." Elf managed to keep one eye on him as she pulled cereal, bowls and mugs from the cupboards.

"Great." He stretched his arms overhead, taking advantage of the temporary freedom she allowed him. "What's on the agenda for today?"

She shot a glare at him. The dishes hit the table with more force than necessary, giving him a very strong clue that she didn't enjoy his captivity any more than he did. Or maybe she needed some caffeine to take the edge off.

A stainless steel teakettle on the stove whistled. She cut off the shrill noise. "I don't know how to make coffee, so if you want some, you're out of luck. You'll have to make do with tea."

"I'll manage, thanks."

She started what looked to him like an elaborate chemistry experiment. Had to be more bother than making a pot of coffee, but he wasn't about to point that out to her.

The woman was a pile of contradictions.

Today she barely resembled the Elf of yesterday. The body jewelry was gone. She wore an oversized, black polo-style shirt and baggy khaki pants. He did recognize the spiked belt she'd been wearing the first time he saw her. Was this just another costume? What would it take to get to know the real person?

She settled on the chair across from him. "My cell phone still isn't getting a signal. If we get to an area with a live zone or a working land line, how likely are we to actually reach your boss?"

"Before Monday? I'd say fifty-fifty. We could always leave a message."

"Won't do much good. She won't be able to reach us." Elf sighed, leaned back in her chair and tugged on her hair.

"Did you get any sleep?"

"I've had less." The soft beep-beep-beep of a timer dragged her out of her chair and back to the teapot.

She'd never make it through the weekend at this rate. Exhaustion slowed her reactions and dulled the light in her eyes.

Considering the circumstances, he should be glad. His chances of escaping improved incrementally with each hour she went without rest.

Rather than figuring out how to take advantage of that edge, his interest had shifted from escaping her to concern for her. She'd gotten under his skin.

The realization jolted him back to a trail of thought he'd rather avoid. The instant physical reaction he had every time she came near was one thing. That he could handle. Attraction on any other level—that was another situation altogether.

He didn't know her nearly well enough to risk getting involved. He'd already been down that road, and knew the route by heart. It hadn't been a pleasant trip.

Elf returned to the table with the cheery yellow teapot and a matching sugar bowl. Another circuit around the kitchen and she added milk, cereal and silverware to the selection.

She finally slumped into the chair, filled her mug with tea and doctored it with milk and sugar. Her scowl dared him to comment and he wisely opted for silence until she finished her first mug and started on a second serving.

"Okay, Cabrini, I'm starting to feel human, so out with it."

"What?"

"Being the secret agent guy, I imagine you've got all sorts of advice for how I should run this little operation."

He nodded. "Since you asked. First off, I'd recommend a healthier diet." He pushed at the bag of Golden Crisp cereal. "Or did you wind up with someone else's grocery cart?"

"I happen to like puffed wheat, and I don't see any difference between my adding the sugar or the manufacturer preapplying it for me. Except I don't have to worry about the proportions."

"Uh-huh. What about exercise?"

"I hate it. But I try to do something physical most days. Swimming, kickboxing. Today—" she gave him a narrow-eyed look "—pounding on a heavy bag holds a certain appeal. Too bad I had to settle for a run."

"What about a social life?"

She gaped at him. "What, so now you're going to tell me that your agency is really just a facade for an escort service?"

He chuckled. "I doubt that Kat McKay has ever been accused of that. Although it does raise interesting possibilities."

"What am I gonna do with you, Cabrini?" She shook her head.

"I can think of several things, but we should probably get to know each other better before any of them is going to happen."

A soft pink tinted her cheeks. "What do you propose?"

"Poker."

Milk dribbled from her spoon as she studied him for a moment. A wicked gleam came into her eyes. "You're on."

They made quick work of breakfast. While he did the dishes, she brewed more tea and found a deck of cards.

By mid-morning, they took their game out to the back deck overlooking the lake.

When noon rolled around, he was surprised to learn he'd developed a taste for very strong tea, kid's cereal and verbal sparring.

He'd also discovered Elf had a competitive streak a mile wide.

Dark clouds rolled in, turning the lake reflections a dull gray. The wind picked up, cooling the air. Ripples danced across the water. They moved their game back inside and took a break for a lunch of scrambled eggs and toast.

The first drops of rain spattered against the window as Frank cleared away the dishes under Elf's close supervision. He refilled their glasses with the strong iced tea and settled onto the banquette. "I think it's time we upped the stakes."

"What do you have in mind?"

"You're familiar with that old favorite, strip poker?"

"Forget it, Cabrini." She reached for the deck of cards in his hand.

He held them out of her reach. "Give me a minute here. You haven't even heard what the variation is."

Thunder rumbled in the distance as the storm continued to build.

"Fine, you get one minute. What's this variation?"

"Truth poker. Winner of the hand gets to ask the question, loser has to answer truthfully."

"What kinds of questions?"

"Any topic is fair game. The better the hand, the tougher the question."

She considered it for a bit, never breaking eye contact with him. Finally she nodded. "Okay, you're on." She held out her hand and he passed the cards.

He smothered his grin. There were a half dozen questions he was itching to ask her and this gave him the perfect opportunity. Her competitiveness would drive the stakes up and her integrity would keep her from lying.

The game posed a calculated risk for him. He'd play fair and answer her questions. Trading information for information was standard operating procedure.

There was the possibility that he'd have to reveal more than he'd normally do.

Of course, as she'd pointed out the night before, this wasn't normal.

Elf shuffled the deck as he laid out the rules. "We'll keep this simple, since there's just the two of us. Deal seven cards, we each get one draw. Best five card hand wins. Winner asks the question."

He declined the cut and she dealt. The only sound, as they studied their cards, was the soft tapping of rain against the windows. He drew two cards, she drew one. They laid their hands faceup on the table.

Her three of a kind beat his pair.

"You said you were from the east coast. Where, exactly?"

"Boston, the north end."

"How come you don't sound like it?"

"That's two questions, but we're just getting started, so I'll give it to you." He gathered the cards, shuffled and dealt. "Diction lessons."

She started to ask him why, then stopped. The cards were in play and she'd have to win another hand to satisfy her curiosity.

The next hand fell to him. His pair of jacks beat her high card. "What is your full name?"

"Angela Marie."

"Marie is your last name?"

"That's two questions." A tiny smile tugged at the corner of her mouth.

"I did say 'full name.'"

"True. Okay, my full name is Angela Marie Donovan. Since I didn't answer completely the first time, I'll give you a bonus. My confirmation name is Catherine."

Donovan? Not a unique name in Minneapolis, by any means. However, factoring in that his client's name was Donovan, a possible connection had to be considered. The game took on another level of importance.

Elf gathered the cards, shuffled and dealt. The game fell into a rhythm with information flowing both ways.

He was oldest of six children, the only boy.

She was an only child.

His parents were still alive and still married.

She had been an A student in high school.

He was two years older.

She'd never had a pet.

He'd spent a short period of time in the army, missed seeing any action.

She'd worked her way through college, where she majored in criminal justice.

When his enlistment was up, he joined the ATF for a while, becoming an arson expert before leaving for the private sector.

She loved cars and had done most of the engine work on Rusty herself, with a little help from an old high school friend.

Thunder rumbled overhead and lightning flashed in the darkening sky. The rain fell in sheets as the storm intensified. They ignored all of it, except to turn on lights.

Frank laid down four of a kind, the best hand he'd had since they started playing. She tossed a pitiful pair of deuces on the card pile.

He had to take advantage of the opportunity. He studied her, gauging her mood and wondering what her reaction might be.

"What are you waiting for?" Her eyes narrowed.

"Just working out what would be the best question."

"I suppose you feel obligated to make it deeply personal."

"Personal?" He leaned back and crossed his arms. "Hadn't thought of it quite like that, although it does open up a whole 'nother avenue of possibilities, doesn't it?"

"Just remember, Cabrini. It swings both ways."

"It'll take quite a bit to top four of a kind."

"Doesn't mean it can't be done."

He shrugged off the warning. "I'm willing to risk it. But I still need to figure out what the question will be. I could ask about your first boyfriend." His eyes lingered on her lips. "Or first kiss. But those seem like a waste of a good hand. Maybe…" He let the unfinished sentence hang in the air between them.

"What?"

"First time you had sex?"

Hot color flooded her cheeks.

He was surprised to find himself seriously considering the question. Images of her naked, rumpled and sated, set his blood on a hot streak to his crotch.

Dangerous territory. He drained his glass of iced tea. *Very dangerous territory.*

If he wasn't careful, he would lose track of what he was supposed to be doing—finding an arsonist and murderer. This woman interfered with that, on more than one level.

The investigation took priority. He needed to get back on task. He needed to find out what, if any, connection Elf might have to his client.

"No." He shook his head. "Questions about sex should probably wait for a royal flush."

Her blush deepened and he almost laughed. A bounty

hunter who didn't swear and who blushed at the mention of sex.

"Keep it up, Cabrini, and I'll be getting the handcuffs."

He raised his hands in surrender. "Okay, okay. Then how about you telling me who Dex is?"

The slight hesitation of her hands as she gathered the cards hinted that he'd surprised her with that question. "You sure you want to waste four of a kind on that?"

"Why not?"

"You'll be disappointed." She shrugged but he didn't buy her casual air. She was stalling.

"My hand to waste."

"Okay, then." She started dealing the next hand. "Dex is an old family friend. He was my father's partner and has been something of a surrogate father to me."

"That's all?"

"I told you you'd be disappointed." She wouldn't look him in the eyes.

"He's not your client?"

She shook her head and picked up her cards. "Uh-uh, Cabrini. One question per hand—those were your rules."

They alternated low winning hands for the next few rounds. By tacit agreement, they stuck with questions about favorite colors, foods and the like.

Another hand fell to him. The full house, queens over tens, was good enough to bump the questions back up a notch. Asking Dex's full name would reveal too much. He could try for her father's line of business. Or...

"Tell me about your mother."

Thunder growled, louder and closer.

Elf sipped from her nearly empty glass, then got up for a refill. "That's not a question."

"Okay. What is your mother like?"

She stood at the counter, wiping condensation from her glass, not looking at him. "She's…fragile." Outside, wind pushed through the tree branches, sending leaves and twigs flying through the air. "I like to remember her when she was happy and always smiling. That was the best time."

"How old were you?"

"Ten."

"Why doesn't she smile anymore?"

She shook her head. "That would be a third question."

"It was a good hand." He pushed a little, testing her reaction.

"Not good enough."

"Okay." Advance and retreat. He'd gotten some information and could afford to wait for another opportunity before pushing again. He shuffled, dealt and deliberately threw away a pair of aces.

She laid out her hand—a pair of queens. "How long have you been on this case?"

"Two months."

She won the next hand without any help from him. "What are you investigating?"

"Insurance fraud."

"That's vague."

"When you have something more than three of a kind, we'll talk."

He laid down the next winning hand. "What about your father?"

She shook her head.

"I beat your pair."

"You're too vague. Ask a specific question."

Time for the next push. "When did he walk out on you and your mother?"

"He did not walk out on us." Her voice trembled with fierce undertones.

Lightning split the sky and a crash of thunder rattled the kitchen window behind his head. Electricity crackled in the air.

Her eyes snapped with anger. "He was a police officer, killed in the line of duty by an arsonist who'd skipped out on bail."

That explained a few things. He didn't like how it was all connecting, either.

Topping it all off was one detail he'd like to verify as soon as possible, because it really mucked up his investigation.

If his suspicion proved correct, The Diamond Group's client and Elf's mother were one and the same.

Maryam Donovan.

Chapter 6

Angel gathered the cards and began shuffling. She needed the mindless action to get her emotions back under control. The cards slapped onto the table like small-caliber pistol reports as she dealt out the next hand.

Cabrini's question hadn't been unexpected, but his assumption hurt. She knew her father hadn't been a saint. He'd been all too human. And he'd been a great dad. He hadn't deserved to die like that.

When Cabrini laid down another winning hand, she braced herself for his question.

"What was your worst date?"

She blinked, surprised. "Going soft, Cabrini?" Why wasn't he asking a follow-up question?

"You opened the topic when I had the four of a kind. It got me to wondering about your social life."

"Nonexistent would be a good adjective."

"You don't date? Ever?"

"Not if I can help it. My friends have set me up on occasion, but…" She waved a hand in dismissal. "Tina especially has tried, but she mostly comes up with cops, and that's never gonna work."

"Why not?"

She pushed the cards towards him. He'd have to win the answer to that question if he really wanted to know.

His pair beat her hand of ten over nothing. "Why not?"

"You really want to know?"

He nodded.

"Fine. I don't do casual. If I'm going to get serious about a man, he better stick around for the long run. Law enforcement, military—most men in uniform—have a tendency to leave. They seem to lose interest real fast when they realize I can match them story for story about saving the world from scumbags."

"Bet you never threw a game to let a guy win."

She snorted.

"Didn't think so. Good."

She held the next winning hand. Four queens should buy her some information. "About your investigation…who's your client?"

"Sorry, Elf." He tossed his cards on the table and leaned back. "Some things are off-limits. I'm sure you understand the need for client confidentiality."

"We haven't established proof that you have a client. Or that you even are a detective." If he was going to use her words against her, he'd better be able to back them with more than a story.

"True."

"In fact—" she leaned back in her chair and mirrored his posture "—I have no way of knowing if anything you've told me bears any resemblance to the truth."

"Also true."

"Impasse."

"So it would seem." Cabrini gathered the cards into a neat stack.

Distant thunder signaled an end to the afternoon storm. "Any bright suggestions?"

The whispery shuffling of cards filled the silence. He never looked at his hands, concentrating instead on her. "Do you suppose the storm has improved your phone's reception?"

"Probably not, but it's worth a try." She retrieved the phone from the charger and flipped it open. "No signal."

"How far do you think we'd have to go to get one?"

"Not far. I think there's a tower fairly close. We just need to get out of the trees. We could walk to the end of the drive and see if that makes a difference."

"I'm willing if you are."

"What good will it do? It's Saturday. Who are we going to call?"

He laid the deck of cards on the table and spread them in a tidy arch. "You'll call Information and get the phone number for The Diamond Group in Washington, D.C. That way, you don't have to waste time suspecting any number I call of being a setup."

She nodded. His logic ran along the same lines as hers. "Then what?"

"Then you call the agency. At that point, you're going to have to trust me, Elf. I've got a code that'll connect me to the owner's private line. Even if it is the weekend, Kat will answer."

"You lied."

"No."

"Ah, yeah. You said you couldn't reach her."

"No, I said she would have left the office, which is true. And that she might have her line forwarded. Also true, provided you have the code. I do."

"Okay. Fine. But until then, we don't go anywhere without the handcuffs."

He slid out from behind the table. "What are we waiting for?"

The temperature had dropped further with the storm's passage. Puddles stood out on the gravel road. She pulled on her thick-soled tennis shoes and a sweatshirt, then snapped the cuffs over their wrists.

The heavy rain had washed the air, leaving behind a mix of fresh pine and rich, woodsy smell. Every scent seemed magnified, including that of the man walking beside her. Their shackled hands swung companionably. Nerves all along her arm tingled with awareness of Cabrini.

The afternoon had played out in a far more interesting manner than she had expected. The exchange of information had been primarily casual, with each of them slipping in more in-depth questions when the opportunity arose.

Cabrini was nothing like the men she usually met in her line of work. Under any other circumstances, she'd be very attracted to him.

The possibility should bother her. Whatever the attraction between them, it wouldn't be long-term. One way or another, he'd leave and she'd be alone.

She wanted the kind of relationship she remembered her parents having. There had been laughter, hugs, whispered exchanges. She remembered how her mother's eyes had danced with happiness.

That happiness had been destroyed by her father's death.

No, emotional entanglement wasn't worth the pain of loss when it ended. She'd done well to keep clear of all that.

As they walked, she held her cell phone in her hand,

watching the signal. The trees thinned closer to the county road, and the symbols flickered. When they reached the end of the drive, the reception held steady. She dialed Information for the D.C. number and accepted the connection.

A car passed them as they stood on the shoulder, the engine noises soon fading into birdsong.

Somewhere in the distance, a couple of all-terrain vehicles chased through the woods. The Department of Natural Resources hadn't finalized the ban on ATVs in this area yet, and vacationers were squeezing in every last ride they could.

Her phone line clicked and a voice mail system picked up. She listened long enough to confirm she'd reached the right number, then handed the phone to Cabrini.

He punched in a series of numbers, then handed the phone back to her.

Two rings later, a woman's voice answered. "Kathleen McKay. This better be good."

"Ms. McKay, my name is Angela Donovan. I'm a bail bond enforcer in Minneapolis. I have a man in custody who claims to work for you."

"Minneapolis?"

"Yes, ma'am."

Frank followed the conversation easily, fairly confident he could predict most of the information Kat would provide in response to Elf's questions.

He knew exactly when Elf began to believe he was who, and what, he said he was. Her shoulders relaxed and she studied him with unflinching directness. When he winked at her and mouthed, *Told you so,* she shook her head and responded with a warm, full smile, dimple and all.

His stomach did a weird little dip and roll.

The conversation finally wound down, and she handed the phone to him. Kat spent no time on pleasantries, opting instead for her usual direct approach.

"A bounty hunter?"

"So it would seem. You vouched for me?"

"I told her you were disreputable and she shouldn't trust you any farther than she could throw you."

"She already figured out that much."

"Smart woman. I look forward to reading your report on how she got the better of you."

"Yeah. I'm sure you'll find it real entertaining." He didn't look forward to writing that part of the report. "With a little cooperation, I might be able to include her client's name. She hasn't revealed his identity to me yet."

"You're sure she has one?" Kat's tone turned serious.

"Yes."

"Have you told her who we're working for?"

"No."

"Do you think they're related?"

"That seems to be a strong probability."

"Has your investigation been compromised?"

"I don't think so, ma'am, but I intend to find out. As soon as we get back to civilization."

Kat's sigh came over the phone line. "I just sent a team to Hawaii. It'll be a week, at least, before I can get reinforcements to you."

"Not to worry. I'm sure Ms. Donovan will be more than willing to work with me."

The line went silent for a moment. "Keeping her close is probably a good idea."

Frank thought so, too, but for very different reasons than his boss implied. He laced his fingers through Elf's and held tight as she tried to tug free.

Angel gave up after the first try. It wasn't like she

could get very far away from him anyway. Not until she got the cuffs off. She had little choice but to tolerate the intimate touch.

He ended his portion of the conversation and handed the phone back to her. "Well, are you satisfied?"

"That you're a private investigator? Yes."

"So we can lose the bracelets?"

She nodded. The cell phone chimed.

"And head back to the Cities?"

The phone display showed the voice mail icon. She pressed a few buttons. "There's a message from earlier this morning."

Dex's voice played back in her ear. "Angela, I'm hoping you get this message before it's too late. I've made some arrangements and will be at the cabin sometime tomorrow. Stay put, and we'll get this matter dealt with very soon."

"What?" Cabrini prompted when she stowed the phone in her pocket.

"We're staying."

"I need to get back to Minneapolis."

"Hot date?"

"No, just my job."

That stopped her for a minute. "We can't go back yet. That message was from my client. He's going to meet us here tomorrow. Have a little patience, and I'm sure all your questions will be answered."

"Why is he coming here? Why don't we go back and meet him in Minneapolis?"

"Because he said to stay here." She tugged on her hair. "I don't know. I wish I had a better idea of what was going on."

"So do I." He lifted their linked hands. "But first, why don't you dig out the key and undo these?"

"No key."

His hand convulsed around hers. "Not funny, Elf."

"Not trying to be, Cabrini. I didn't bring the key."

"Why the hell not?"

"I wasn't going to take the chance you'd try to wrestle it away from me."

He pulled her close, tucking their cuffed wrists behind her back. "You mean like this?" He began to pat her down, searching her pockets. She struggled against him for a few seconds, then stilled as his frisking turned to caresses.

The rain-freshened air mingled with the scent of his warm skin, surrounding her with an intoxicating blend. He tightened his arm around her waist, snuggling her closer, until nothing but a breath separated them.

"Or maybe you mean this."

She tensed, expecting him to exert his dominance with a controlling sort of kiss. Instead, he dipped his head and brushed his lips over hers. Soft. Once, twice. Then he nipped and nibbled at her lower lip.

Her breath escaped in a shuddering sigh.

A passing car honked, breaking the mood, saving her from his next onslaught. She stepped away from him, knowing the only reason she could do so was because he allowed it. Raking a hand through her hair, she turned back to the driveway.

"Let's get back to the cabin." She started walking, hoping he'd follow and not use the handcuffs to drag her back and force her to negotiate.

He fell into step beside her, lacing his fingers through hers once more, and didn't say a word.

Blessed be for small favors. She needed some quiet time to figure out what had just happened. Between her reactions to his kiss and the phone conversation with his employer, she had a lot on her mind to sort through.

The easy stuff first—it seemed he really was legit.

But she still didn't know the specifics of his investigation or who his client might be. Without that information, she couldn't begin to guess why Dex thought it necessary for her to hold Cabrini hostage in the north woods. "Will you tell me who your client is?"

"I can't. Not yet, anyway."

She shrugged. She hadn't really expected him to change his mind, but a girl could hope.

He gave her hand a little squeeze. "What about you? Will you tell me?"

She shook her head. "I need to talk to him, first."

Cabrini pulled her to a stop. "You can't tell him who I work for."

"Look, it's obvious there's some kind of mistake. He only knows that you're hiding behind an alias and digging around in the past. That'd make anyone suspicious. Once he knows the truth, we can put this whole thing to rest."

"No. Not until you tell me who your client is."

"Not until he's given me the okay to reveal his identity." Impatience sharpened her voice.

"I'm going to find out tomorrow, when he gets here."

"So it won't kill you to wait a few more hours to find out, then, will it?"

"Are you dizzy yet? 'Cause I'm getting there." He started walking again. "Come on, let's get back to the cabin before the mosquitoes come out in full force and carry me away."

She took a cleansing breath. Frustration and confinement didn't suit him very well. She didn't like it much herself. A change of scenery might do them both good. "If you promise to behave yourself, maybe we could go into town for supper."

"Someplace with real vegetables on the menu?"

The hope in his voice had her considering sticking

her tongue out at him. "Hey, at least you didn't go hungry and you got plenty of calcium. With big bones like you've got, you probably need all the help you can get."

They climbed the steps to the front porch of the cabin. He reached in front of her to open the door. She breezed past him, only to stumble to a halt just inside the entry.

"What is it?" He kept his voice low.

"I'm not sure." She looked around the entry. "Something doesn't feel right."

Nothing looked out of order, but there was something in the air that hadn't been there when they left for their walk.

He nodded. "We need to get these cuffs off. Where's the key?"

Angel didn't answer him. She edged her way around the kitchen to peek into the living room. As she looked for something that would explain the hairs standing up on the nape of her neck, she slid the flattened spike from her belt. Slipping it into the handcuff, she released the ratchet, freeing Frank's hand.

He grabbed her wrist and lifted it to get a look at her handy little pick, then raised a questioning eyebrow at her.

She shrugged as she snapped the empty cuff around her wrist and returned the pick to her belt.

They both rubbed the backs of their necks, mirror images of each other. Then he brushed a hand across the nape of her neck, sending little waves of heat chasing down her spine to collide with the sense of danger lodged between her shoulder blades. She ignored both, and nodded, silently acknowledging that she also had the uneasy feeling something was about to happen.

She signaled for him to check the main floor as she worked her way up the stairs.

Nothing seemed amiss in any of the rooms. She retrieved her Airweight from the gun safe in her dresser and met him by the sliding glass patio door.

"Anything?" she whispered.

He pointed at the door. The screen door stood halfway open. About an inch of space showed between the heavy glass slider and the doorjamb.

A noise came from the corner of the patio. She had her gun out and ready in a heartbeat.

Pushing the slider open a little farther, she slipped outside. The noise continued, and she crept to the edge of the wood deck.

The last step down to the lake path squeaked beneath her foot. A metallic crash rang out in answer.

She raised her gun into position as she swung around the corner of the cabin. Sunlight broke through the last clouds and bounced off the dull metal of the garbage can laying tipped on its side. Two raccoons scurried back into the woods.

She sagged against the side of the house as she lowered her revolver.

Cabrini sidled up beside her. "Local wildlife?"

She nodded. "Looks like it. It seems early for them to be out. I'm going to check around the perimeter, just to be sure." She pushed away from the wall. "Could you—"

"Take care of trash duty?" Cabrini heaved a deep sigh. "That seems to be my main use these days."

"Buck up, Cabrini. You could turn into what most women dream of."

"What?"

"A man who cleans up after himself."

He crossed his arms and looked her over. "Is that what you want, Elf?"

"Do I strike you as being like most women?" She

set off down the path. His chuckle followed her on the breeze, sending desire rippling across her stomach.

Most women probably wouldn't look twice at someone with Cabrini's rough appearance. Sometimes she wished she was more like most women. The more she got to know about him, the more she grew to like him.

Ten minutes later, she returned to the cabin. Everything had been cleaned up and the trashcan was secured in place. Cabrini stood on the porch, waiting for her.

"Thanks for picking up." She sank onto a patio chair. "Did you find anything?"

"There were a few ATV tracks, but that's all. Am I going paranoid?"

"If you are, I'm keeping you company."

She rested her head in her hands and gave her scalp a good scratching. "This is nuts. No one knows we're here, and if they did, why would they come after us, anyway?"

"Your mystery client sent *you* after *me*."

"I told you, I'm sure it's just a misunderstanding."

He sat in the chair next to hers. "So, what do you want to do?"

"Eat." She relaxed against the cushions and closed her eyes against the lowering sun. "Eating would be good."

"Are you cooking?"

"No. I wouldn't think of subjecting you to that sort of torture again." She frowned at him. "Do you promise to behave?"

"I always behave. Just not always very well."

"Got it. Okay, if we go into town, do you promise to be on your best behavior and not make any attempt to escape?"

"What do I get if I do?"

"The pleasure of dining at a surprisingly nice steak

house not too far from here. If you're really good, I might even let you have some wine or other alcoholic beverage of your choice."

"Are there vegetables?"

"I imagine there might be a head of iceberg lettuce floating around the kitchen. They could probably come up with a decent salad. If you don't expect much."

"Sounds great." He crossed his heart and held up his hand. "I solemnly swear that I will be charming, congenial and cordial. I will stick beside you, no matter what."

Stick beside her. The concept held a certain attraction. And nothing would come of it. She smiled and shook her head. "Don't push it, Cabrini, or I'll suspect you of trying to distract me. Let's get changed and head into town."

Frank, dressed in a fresh pair of jeans and a clean T-shirt, watched in awe as Elf came down the stairs.

She had completely transformed her appearance once again. Long, curly black hair cascaded over her shoulders and down her back. Brown contacts hid the blue eyes he'd admired all day. And her clothes… His mouth went dry.

Holy hot pants.

An oversized, white shirt, left unbuttoned enough to reveal teasing glimpses of the curves underneath, had him torn between buttoning her up to the neck or undoing the shirt completely. The stiletto heels of her red shoes and her short jean skirt left an impression that her legs ended somewhere around next Wednesday.

He let loose with a wolf whistle.

"Get over it, Cabrini."

"It is you. I wondered for a second." He shook his head. "When you say you're going to change, you don't fool around."

She couldn't possibly have any idea of the effect she would have on men seeing her for the first time. They'd be hitting on her all night long and he'd probably end up hitting one of them, just for the principle.

He was about to say so when he caught the knowing look in her disguised eyes and the quirk of her eyebrow. "You want to cause problems, don't you?"

"Why, Mistah Cabrini, I can't imagine what you mean."

"Like hell you can't. Why a disguise?"

"Because I never leave home without it. Just like I don't leave home without this." She held up a credit card and some folded cash before slipping them into her front pocket. "Or this." She slid her driver's license and a lipstick tube into the other pocket. "Or this." She lifted her skirt just enough to reveal the edge of a garter holding her cell phone in place high on her thigh.

He had to swallow a couple times before he could get his voice working again. "Ever try carrying a purse?"

"Too much bother. I always forgot it someplace. Besides, the only thing I carry that's too big for a pocket is my handy Smith & Wesson Bodyguard Airweight."

"And where do you plan to tuck that?"

"Rusty's trunk. I like to keep it handy, but most businesses don't allow guns on the premises."

Of course. He'd been foolish to think the afternoon's exchanges had made a difference in their situation. She was still on the job. So was he. "Why the disguise, Elf?"

She flipped her hair over her shoulder. "I have my reasons."

"Enlighten me."

"Maybe later."

"Maybe now."

She pouted. "You're just being a big ol' spoilsport."

"Give it up, Elf. You're forgetting we've played cards all afternoon. I know you too well for the southern-belle bit to be effective."

"Fuhgeddaboudit." She switched to a Jersey accent. "I suppose you think this is better?"

He shook his head.

"No?" She shifted accents again, and sounded straight out of the movie *Fargo.* "Oh, yah, sure. Well, you know, I suppose since we're up nort' I should sound like them folks, then, huh?"

"Why the costume?"

"Distraction." She brushed past him with a chicka-boom swing of her hips that had his libido, and other parts, standing at attention. "Is it working?"

"You're killing me, Elf."

Her throaty laugh scrambled his thoughts. "Care to take a ride, big guy?"

Oh, yeah, it was working, all right. Too well.

Chapter 7

Dinner, as it turned out, was quite pleasant. Nobody hit on Elf, and Frank occupied himself trying to decipher the puzzle she presented. Angel Donovan fascinated him and frustrated him and he wanted to get to know more about her. He wanted to know *everything* about her.

They ate and laughed and he coaxed her out onto the miniscule dance floor once. Once was enough.

She fit in his arms like she'd been custom-tailored for him.

He was heading for dangerous ground and he didn't care.

They returned to the cabin well after midnight. The moonless night wrapped around them, serenading them with the frog-and-cricket chorus of the woods.

He followed her up the porch steps, took the keys from her hand and unlocked the door. "You know, Elf, this is the closest I've come to a date in a long time."

"Really?"

"Um-hmm." He brushed her hair over her shoulder and cupped her cheek. "I'm out of practice. What comes next?"

He felt more than saw the tiny shake of her head. "I'm probably more out of practice than you are."

"Interesting." The fact that she didn't date much pleased him in a strange way.

He enjoyed being with her, regardless of how it had all begun. He didn't know where it would lead, but was willing to go along for the ride for a little longer. "Well, I'm pretty sure—" he stepped closer "—a good-night kiss is still customary."

With her high heels, she stood nearly as tall as him and he didn't have to bend very far.

He paused, waited to see if she would pull away. Her soft breath teased his lips, lured him closer.

The first brush of his lips on hers set his blood humming through his veins. He played with the sensations, experimenting with the pressure and placement of his mouth on hers, letting the hunger build in a sweet torture before advancing to the next step.

He teased her lips, tracing their outline with the tip of his tongue, tasting the lingering flavor of her chocolate dessert. When he reached the limits of his patience for that, he deepened the kiss.

Her arms wound around his shoulders and he pulled her closer, matching her length to his as he leaned against the door. The heat built.

Each time he'd kissed her, it had been different. The desire to know her better, to get closer, to taste more of her, grew with each experience.

A film of perspiration spread across his back and, with it, reality intruded. Hot as his desire might be, there was something else going on.

He loosened his hold on her enough to reach behind him and touch the door. It was unnaturally hot. The doorknob was even hotter.

A branch cracked somewhere nearby. Splinters of wood bit into his cheek.

Not a branch, realization hit. Gunshot. The bullet had come damn close.

He tightened his arm around Elf's waist and dragged her off the porch, racing to get to the shelter of the car.

Another crack of gunfire. Glass shattered and the world exploded.

The blast knocked them to the ground. He twisted to cover her body with his, protecting her from falling debris. Something hit him in the back with the force of a fist.

It was over in a matter of seconds.

Flames engulfed the cabin.

In the distance, an angry mechanical buzz disappeared in the roar of the growing fire.

"Holy mother of—" He stood and helped Elf to her feet. "Are you okay?"

She nodded, speechless, as she took in the devastation.

He pulled the car door open and shoved her behind the steering wheel. "Come on. We're getting out of here."

She nodded again, fumbled the key into the ignition. He slid into the passenger seat as the engine roared to life. As he pulled the door shut, she shoved the car into gear and peeled away, spraying gravel in their wake.

At the end of the long driveway, she slammed on the brakes. "We can't just leave. We have to do something, call the fire department, get them out here. The whole woods could catch on fire."

"Which would suit whoever set that fire, I'm sure."

She looked at him, anger and fear growing in her eyes. "What are you talking about?"

"Get on that cell phone of yours and call nine-one-one, Elf. You're right—we need the fire department ASAP. The local law enforcement would be good, too. Once they're done, I'll be real interested in what the fire investigator has to say."

"You think it was deliberate?"

He nodded. "Make the call, then we'll talk."

She called in the fire, then pulled her car onto the far shoulder of the road, got out and walked around to the passenger side. The car door creaked as she pulled it open. "Okay, now explain why you think this is arson."

Muscle twinges and shoulder pain accompanied his movements as he stood next to the car. "Do you know what a backdraft is?"

"I've read about it, but can't seem to keep the term straight."

"A fire smolders in an enclosed area, just waiting for a fresh air supply. When it gets that air, it explodes, literally."

"Like the cabin just did."

"Right. Our fire had a little help in renewing its oxygen. Whoever it was missed on the first shot."

"First…" She slumped against Rusty's back fender, arms crossed. "I heard it. But out here…it didn't register."

"Took me a second, too. The bullet hitting the door next to my head helped. The second shot opened a window and—" he clapped his hands together "—bang."

"Backdraft."

Lights strobed in the distance and the sound of sirens began to fill the air. "That was fast."

"Dispatch said we were the second call."

"Neighbors?"

"They didn't say. I thought I heard an ATV—it could have been the rider." She glanced at him. "This stinks like last week's sauerkraut."

"No argument there."

The fire engine skidded around the sharp turn into the driveway. The fire chief's SUV followed hard behind.

The county sheriff's patrol car skidded to a stop, blocking the drive.

"Methuselah," Elf muttered.

"What?"

"This guy. He's been sheriff since the first Ice Age."

"He knows you?"

"Not this version. It's been years."

"Let's keep it that way." Frank spoke in a low tone. "I don't think hanging around here is good for our health so let's not give him any reasons to keep us."

The sheriff stood next to his car, one hand resting on the butt of his gun, the other aiming his spotlight at them. The bright beam trailed over the Mustang, then settled on Elf. "You the folks that called it in?"

Frank draped an arm around Elf's shoulders as they faced the peace officer.

"Nooo. I pulled over for just a second?" Elf waved her arms vaguely and slipped a question mark into every sentence. "All of a sudden? We heard this big, ya know, noise?"

"What were you doing stopping here? You know the owner of this place?"

Elf tried to pull away. Frank squeezed her shoulder, pulling her in front of him and wrapping his arms around her. "Was that some kind of party house?" he asked.

"You from around here?" The sheriff shifted the light to Frank's face.

"Nah. I'm not. But Chris, here," he smoothed her hair away from her neck. "She tells me she comes through here all the time. I just wanted to see some of the countryside."

The sheriff's spotlight moved back to Elf. "Did you see anybody?"

"Nooo?"

Frank tickled her neck with his beard. She giggled right on cue, adding a little more ditz to her performance.

The sheriff studied them for a moment. "Well, keep driving. The fire crew's got their hands full. We don't need spectators getting in the way."

"Okie, then." Elf gave a little wave of her hand.

They wasted no time getting back in the car. Under the guise of giving her a kiss, Frank leaned close and said, "Step on it, *Chris.*"

She complied, making a big show of checking for nonexistent traffic and waving to the sheriff as she pulled onto the road.

Through the rear window, Frank watched the sheriff pull out a cell phone. His spotlight bobbed for a moment, then trained on them and held steady as they drove away.

Ten miles down the road, Angel's cell phone vibrated, jerking her attention away from their dark surroundings. She pulled to the side of the road.

"As much as I'd love a quick make-out session, I'd really prefer that we keep going."

"Zip it, Cabrini." She hiked her skirt up a little to pull the phone from its garter holster.

Cabrini's soft whistle would have earned him a backhanded swat but she was too busy tugging her skirt back into place and sliding out of the car.

A chill slithered down her spine when she saw her mother's phone number on the screen. "Corie? Is something wrong? Has something happened?"

"Angela?" Her mother's voice came through the receiver.

"Mom?"

"Oh, sweetie, is it really you?"

"Of course it is. Who else would it be?" She began pacing alongside the car.

"Thank heaven it's not too late," Maryam whispered.

"Mom, it's nearly two in the morning. Why are you calling?"

"You're all right." Her mother's voice broke on a soft sob. "You aren't hurt, are you?"

"No, Mom, I'm fine. What's going on?"

"He said there'd been an explosion.... It didn't make sense—it's all confused.... It sounded like when your father... I can't live through that again."

Her own memories of that time clamped an iron fist around her heart. Neither of them could survive that sort of devastation a second time.

"Mom? Mom, it's okay. I'm okay. Nothing has happened." She stopped pacing. Covering her ear, focusing all her attention on the distraught woman on the other end, she ignored her own remembered loss and worked to calm her mother.

After numerous reassurances, her mother calmed down enough to hand the phone to Corie.

"What the Frankfurt is that all about? Who told her I was dead?"

"He didn't say that, exactly. He said there was a fire and you were missing. She jumped from there to..."

"The only logical conclusion in her mind." Angel sank against Rusty's rear fender.

"You're really okay?"

"Yes, I'm fine." She rubbed the back of her neck, pushing at the edge of her wig. "Corie, who called with that information?"

"Mr. Dexter."

Chilling anger threaded through her veins. "Why would he do that to her? How could he call in the middle of the night and say something like that?"

"He didn't call—he came here."

She pushed away from the car. "Put him on the phone." Her voice shook with the effort it took not to shout.

"He's already left. He got a phone call and took off a few minutes ago."

"Corie, take care of Mom. See if you can get her to calm down. Maybe try calling Dr. Brenna's service to see if she can talk to Mom. I don't know what's going on, but I'm going to find out. I'll be in touch as soon as I can, in the morning."

"It would be better if you came home."

"I know." Her throat ached. "And I will, as soon as I possibly can."

She cut the connection and dialed another number.

"Dexter here."

"How dare you do that to my mother." Anger throbbed through her voice.

"Angela?"

She began pacing again. "Yes, it's me. What the hell were you thinking to tell my mother I was missing?"

"Angela…I can't believe it's you. When the sheriff called to say the cabin was burning, I thought… I can't begin to tell you what I thought."

"Whatever it was, it wasn't very smart."

"How did you know…? Are you at your mother's?"

"No, she called me."

"Why would she do that if she—"

"Because that's what she does when she's upset or has a bad feeling. She calls me to make sure I'm okay. Too bad you didn't think to do the same thing before dropping a bomb on her in the middle of the night."

"Where are you?"

Something in his voice triggered a caution alarm in her brain. She stopped pacing. "I'm a safe distance from all the action."

"Cabrini?"

"He's here with me."

"That's good to know. Are you coming home, then? I'm sure Maryam will want to actually see you before she believes you aren't hurt."

"I'll be there as soon as possible."

"Good. We'll be watching for you."

She ended the call and met Cabrini's inquisitive look.

"He as good as told Mom I was dead." She hated the pain that must have caused her mother. Tears burned the back of her eyes and closed her throat. She started pacing again, not watching where she stepped.

Cabrini caught her when her narrow heel turned on the gravel shoulder. "Easy, Elf." He folded her in his arms.

It felt so safe there, sheltered by his strength. Since the day her father died, she'd had to be the strong one. Now, she wanted to sink into Cabrini's protection and hide. The thought stiffened her spine and she stepped away.

He let her go, but kept a gentle hold on her elbows. "Tell me what happened."

She related the *Reader's Digest* version, ending with, "Something's not right. We need to know what's going on."

"You won't get any argument from me. Who talked to your mother?"

"Dex."

"How did he already know about the fire?"

"He said the sheriff called him, but something's not adding up." She strode to the rear of the car and opened the trunk.

Cabrini followed.

She shoved a flashlight into his hand. "Here, hold this." She moved some supplies out of the way and reached to the back of the trunk. "Got it."

She wriggled back out of the trunk and caught Cabrini staring at her backside. "What?"

"Nothing." He held up one hand in surrender. "Enjoying the show, that's all."

Having him ogle her shouldn't bother her. She used her appearance like any other tool of her trade. But the situation with Cabrini wasn't the norm. They'd gotten to know each other as individuals. Her cheeks heated with anger and embarrassment that she had misjudged him, had thought better of him than he deserved. "Well, show's over."

Cabrini wisely chose to ignore her and noticed what she held in her hands. "A police scanner?"

"I figure, if we can't be there, we can at least hear what the locals are saying."

"Any chance you have a first-aid kit in there?"

She pulled a metal box from its corner in the trunk. "Here. Why? You get a splinter or something?"

"Or something." He twisted around some as he looked over his shoulder. "I don't think it's serious, but it hurts like the devil. What does it look like?"

A dark stain covered a large portion of his T-shirt back. She swallowed hard. "Why didn't you say something?"

"Not a lot of opportunity between then and now."

She took the flashlight from him and gave his back a quick once-over. "Take your shirt off."

"I thought you'd never ask."

A blush burned her cheeks. "So I can see how bad it is."

"This is probably not the best place. I can manage for a few more miles." He took the flashlight back. "Let's get the scanner hooked up, then figure out where we can hole up for the first aid."

He fanned the beam of light over the trunk contents. "Looks like a lot of gear."

She slammed the lid.

"Was that a baseball bat?"

"Yes." She got into the car and hooked up the scanner, tuning into a channel that buzzed with chatter.

"Care to share what other bags of tricks you have back there?"

"No. Shut up and listen."

He did, and what they heard sent a chill crawling over her scalp.

...arson suspects. Female, Caucasian, five-nine, bleached blond and blue. Male, Caucasian, six-four, black and blue, heavy beard. They are armed and considered dangerous....

"That's us," she whispered.

He nodded, slid into the passenger seat and snapped his seat belt in place. "Close the door and drive. First chance you get, head north."

"But Mom—"

"Is exactly where they expect you to run."

Her heart sank to the pit of her stomach. "Which makes it the last place I can go."

"I'm sorry, Elf."

She nodded and tromped on the gas pedal. Rusty fishtailed on the gravel shoulder as she pulled back onto the road. When they hit the next county road intersection, she turned north.

"This is wrong," she said. "Just plain wrong."

"Right now, we don't have a choice. We can't go back to Minneapolis yet."

"That's not what I'm talking about. It's everything else. Nothing adds up quite right. How did the fire department get there so quick? Who called it in and why didn't they stick around? How did Dex find out so fast?"

"All good questions. I have one of my own. Who is Dex?"

"I told you." She tightened her grip on the steering wheel. "He's a family friend."

"It's time to come clean, Elf. Everything that's happened seems to circle back to him. Why?"

"Whatever it is, it's not what you're thinking."

"No?"

She drove in silence, wrestling with the implications and wishing she could talk through the situation without betraying client confidentiality.

"Come on, Elf. You've got to level with me. If we'd opened that cabin door, we would be toast right now. I don't think it was an accident. Do you?"

"Vandalism."

"You don't really believe it was random, do you?"

"I can't believe it's anything else."

"Why not?"

"Because anything else… No."

"Say it."

"Because if it was deliberate, Dex is in danger."

Cabrini turned in his seat, a look of disbelief on his face. "How do you figure that?"

"It's his place. If he'd been there, he might have been killed. Since he wasn't—"

"No, we were."

"Since he wasn't there, maybe it's just to warn him off something."

"That doesn't explain the bulletin we just heard."

"The sheriff saw us there. If he suspects the fire wasn't an accident, we're the logical starting point."

"You're forgetting…a lot of things, actually, but one in particular."

"What?"

"Right now, you have long, black hair and brown eyes, not that the sheriff was close enough to make out eye color."

She touched the wig she still wore, then pounded the steering wheel in time to her muttered, "Fridley, Fargo, Fresno."

"I agree. Who is Dex?"

"A family friend."

"Not good enough. Who is he? Full name."

"No."

"Yes. He hired you to find me."

She scowled at him. "What makes you think that?"

"Two plus two, Elf. Dex is your client and he wants us out of the way for some reason."

She shook her head in denial.

"*Us,* Elf. That Attempt To Locate bulletin listed us both as suspects. Someone set the sheriff in that direction. I'm pretty sure I know who. I want to know why, and I want to know now."

"Not Dex."

"Fine, not him. There's some other logical explanation for how he got a call from the sheriff, went to your mother, told her you were missing and left. How long had we been driving before your mother called? Fifteen minutes? Twenty?"

A chill curled in her belly, sending tentacles out to wrap around her heart. *It can't be.*

"You said it yourself." Cabrini didn't let up. "Nothing adds up. And it never will as long as you keep Dex out of the equation."

Bits and pieces shifted, taking on new form and meaning. "He sounded surprised when he heard my voice."

"I'll bet he did."

She struggled with the possibility that Dex wasn't the intended victim of the cabin explosion. If she believed Cabrini... "No. You're wrong. There's something more here. Someone else is involved and is using me to get to Dex."

"Why? What's he into that warrants an attack like that?"

"Politics." She spit the word like a curse. "There are some people not too pleased with his intentions."

"To do what?"

She shook her head.

"Supposedly, I would have met him tomorrow. If he was really going to come to the cabin. So why still try to keep his identity secret? It's not like there's a whole lot I can do with the information under the current circumstances."

"I can't."

"Why?"

"Who's *your* client?" If he wanted her to break confidentiality, he better provide something of equal value in exchange.

"You know I can't tell you that. Not yet."

"Well, there's your answer." She turned up the volume on the scanner and drove.

Frank settled into his seat and waited. Sooner or later, she'd have to face the reality. He had a pretty strong suspicion of who Dex was and it didn't give him any warm fuzzies about her family ties.

The scanner broke into the silence with another bulletin. *Update on prior arson ATL. Suspects seen fleeing the house fire on Quay Lake are driving a '73*

Mustang, red with Minnesota plates, MBW733. Do not approach without backup. They are considered armed and dangerous.

"I didn't happen to notice, Elf. What's the number on your car plates?"

Her hands flexing on the steering wheel gave the only indication that she'd heard his softly voiced question.

"Any idea where we're going?" He kept his tone casual.

"You said turn north. I turned north."

"So...you don't know where we're going?"

"Hell, most probably."

"Cute. Maybe you'd consider pulling over so we can discuss what we're going to do?"

"Soon as I find a place. As you said, the shoulder of the road probably isn't the best place for what I have in mind."

What did she have in mind? Probably nothing along the lines of what he'd been hoping for prior to the rude interruption of an exploding building.

Dark pines and ghostly birch trees flashed by in the night, giving the impression they were driving through a living tunnel. Their surroundings were isolated and intimate. No side roads branched off, and the woods just grew thicker.

"Might be easier to find something if you slowed down."

She shot him a look that left little doubt of her appreciation of his observations. She also let up on the gas, and the speedometer needle dropped below sixty-five.

The tension wasn't doing the pain in his back any good. He forced his muscles to relax. Riding in the passenger seat was an unfamiliar sensation, and not one he found particularly comfortable. Much as he would have preferred it, he didn't even try to convince Elf to let him drive.

The headlights flashed off a series of roadside signs. One indicated a curving road, another showed the silhouette of a leaping deer.

The car continued to slow. Elf muttered something that sounded suspiciously like, "Stay away, little deer."

Another sign came into view. The weathered lettering advertised a campground. An arrow pointed down an overgrown track. Elf spun the wheel and followed the barely visible path.

Frank braced his hand on the roof as they bounced over the washboard ruts. He considered asking her where they were going, but didn't want to risk biting off his tongue. They jounced over another bump and his teeth snapped together. Silence was definitely the best plan for the moment.

The joke of a road curved and opened into a clearing. Elf stopped the car. The headlights blinked out and she turned off the engine.

He waited for her to say something. Silence wrapped around them in the velvet darkness. The sweet scent of grass and trees washed over him on a warm breeze as he rolled down his widow.

The soft click of the dome light switch caught his attention. He turned back to look at the woman who was driving him in directions he wasn't entirely comfortable going.

Her glance skittered away from his. She wasn't comfortable, either. He couldn't blame her. When you were used to working alone, it was unsettling to find yourself shackled with an unwilling partner.

Even more unsettling was finding himself with a partner whose skills perfectly matched his.

Adding to his discomfort was his awareness of her

as a woman. He hadn't come close to getting to know the real person beneath all the disguises. Intellectually, that set off more than a few alarms. Physically, it didn't make a bit of difference. His body responded to her presence with a hunger that left him aching. Judging by her reactions, they were well-matched on that front, as well.

They had better get it out of their systems soon.

Chapter 8

Angel pulled off the wig and ruffled her hair. Time for another disguise. She stretched cramped muscles, reaching to the star-studded sky as she walked to Rusty's trunk.

Cabrini stood by the passenger door, watching her.

Awareness of his presence tingled along her skin. She lowered her arms and tugged at the hem of her skirt. The lack of length hadn't been a problem as long as they were in public. The quiet seclusion of the woods presented her with an altogether different sensation.

Getting Cabrini off her hands couldn't happen too soon for her taste. Letting down her guard around him was a mistake, regardless of how good it felt to just relax and be herself for a change.

Be herself. Sometimes it was hard to remember what that meant. She lived most of her life in one disguise or another. That's how she'd structured her method of operation.

When was the last time she'd been herself anywhere other than within the walls of her mother's home?

Forever ago. The time with Cabrini at the cabin had been an aberration.

No matter. She opened Rusty's trunk. The middle of the night, in the middle of an abandoned campground, was no place to start soul searching. She couldn't afford to let the man disrupt her peace of mind. Not when they were the object of an ATL.

Every town cop, highway patrol and county sheriff would be watching for them. They needed to disappear.

Lucky for them, that's what she did best—disappear behind disguises.

Cabrini came around the end of the car as she draped the wig over the trunk lid, then dug out the flashlight and flicked it on. "Let's get your back cleaned up."

She worked slowly, peeling the shirt away from his wound. He never made a sound as she used the peroxide from the first-aid kit to clean the area. "It's not as bad as it looked."

"Glad to hear it. How much longer do you plan to torture me?"

"A few more minutes should do it. I want to make sure I got everything." She picked up the light and inspected the wound, probing with a gentle touch. "It looks like whatever hit you scraped off skin more than anything else."

She dug through the first-aid kit and pulled out an antibacterial cream. "This is going to sting."

He sucked in a breath at the first contact. "That was an understatement."

"I'm sorry." She swapped the cream for gauze and tape. His skin felt firm and warm beneath her fingers. Smoothing the tape into place came dangerously close to becoming a caress.

She slapped the lid back on the first-aid tin and grabbed the flashlight.

"Make yourself useful." She pushed the flashlight into his hands.

The brightness shining directly at her almost blinded her. She raised one hand to shield her eyes.

"Sorry." He lowered the light. The beam trailed down her body, an extension of his hand, caressing her without touching her.

Their eyes met.

She read hunger in his look. An answering hunger for his touch flashed through her, drew her a step closer. The night whirr of crickets blended into the rushing of her pulse.

In spite of his rough facade, Cabrini held more partner potential than any guy she'd ever dated.

No. She caught herself and stepped back. That path led to disaster. The last thing she needed in her life was a man complicating things. This man, especially.

Whatever his assignment was, it had brought him to Minnesota on a temporary basis. As soon as he completed his job, he'd leave and she'd be alone. Just like she'd always been.

If nothing was going to change, it made no sense to invest any of herself into a relationship that was doomed before it started.

She turned to the open trunk and blindly pushed at the contents.

The light shined on the variety of duffel bags she used to store the tools of her trade. Cabrini stepped in too close and looked over her shoulder.

Her elbow made a direct connection with his diaphragm as she yanked a bag from the back of the trunk. She ignored his muffled "Oof" and pulled her bright yellow toolbox to the top of the pile.

She sat on the edge of the trunk and slipped off her high heels. Cabrini aimed the light at the ground, illuminating her bare feet.

Should've gotten a pedicure. She quashed the thought and curled her toes under.

Armed with pliers and a wrench, she padded barefoot to the front of her car. The cool, damp grass of the overgrown yard soothed her achy feet.

Cabrini trailed after her, keeping a safe distance from her elbows and the heavy metal objects she carried. *Smart man.* He trained the flashlight where she pointed.

Night noises from the woods surrounded them. She ignored the intimacy of the dark and their isolation as she worked. In a matter of minutes, she'd removed the front license plate and returned to the back of her car. The rear plate came off with equal ease, and she tossed both into the bag she'd laid on the ground.

She pulled a set of Wisconsin license plates from the bag and bolted them in place.

"Do you really think switched plates will be enough to throw them offtrack?" Cabrini finally spoke.

"No." She stood, shuffled through a couple of mailing tubes before pulling out one with a black end-cap. "However, Wisconsin plates on a black Mustang just might do the trick."

The end-cap popped off and she shook out the contents. "I have a buddy who does signs, vinyl window appliqués, that sort of stuff. I did a little job for him and he paid me with these."

Half an hour later they stood beside Rusty, newly decked out in removable black vinyl panels, complete with custom cutouts to accommodate the rusted out spots on the car body.

She smiled and gave a satisfied nod at the results.

"You have disguises for your car." Cabrini shook his head. "Everything's a front, isn't it?"

Her smile froze in place. His comment hurt. More than it should have. Except she was so tired of the charade. She stowed her tools and the duffel bag back in the trunk.

Her wig hung like a pennant on the trunk lid. Tears burned her eyes. After that comment of his, she couldn't bring herself to put it on again. She pulled an overnight bag to the top and opened it.

Ignoring Cabrini, she stripped off her shirt and donned a tank top. *Let him look, if he wants. It's the closest he'll ever get.*

The white shirt had taken a beating, but not nearly as much as Cabrini's T-shirt had. He'd protected her from the brunt of the explosion.

He'd protected her.

She hadn't asked him to do that. She didn't need protecting. Not by him or anyone else. That was her job. She did the protecting.

She stashed the wig and her high heels in the bag, and pulled out a navy T-shirt. "Here." She held it out to Cabrini. "You can't go running around half naked."

"Thanks." He pulled it on.

"It probably won't meet your fit standards." The trunk lid slammed shut and she turned. Whatever else she might have said drowned in her mouth. The soft, cotton knit hugged his torso, accenting his physique more than hiding it.

Shanghai. How'm I going to survive this?

Ignoring him seemed the best option. She turned on her heel and rounded the car. The driver's seat welcomed her with its familiar embrace. Reaching under her seat, she pulled out a pair of flip-flop sandals and slipped them on.

Cabrini folded himself into the passenger seat. "I know a few agents who could take lessons from you on going undercover."

She turned the car around and tried to shut out the man sitting beside her. Too close. She'd let him get too close without even realizing it, and now he'd gotten under her skin.

"You have quite a talent for disguises. We've been together for nearly thirty-six hours and I have no clue how much, if any, is the real you."

It came easy when you'd lost your real self. "Thanks." She pushed the word out through clenched teeth.

The leather of the bucket seat creaked as he turned toward her. "It was a professional compliment, Elf."

Professional. She shot a scowl at him.

He settled back in his seat and didn't say anything more until they reached the main road. When he did speak, he kept to the business at hand.

"Any idea where we're going?"

"Vaguely."

"Do you think we could find a motel?"

"Probably."

His sigh blended with the hum of the tires on the road. "If we do come across one, would you consider stopping?"

"Doubtful."

"We could both use some rest."

She raised an eyebrow in disbelief. "Right."

"Seriously. How much sleep have you gotten in the last three days?"

"Enough."

A few miles clicked by in silence before he tried to make conversation again.

"Do you want to talk about it?"

"What?"

"Whatever's eating at you."

Why couldn't he shut up? "I don't know what you're talking about."

"No? Try this on—sex."

If he only knew. "Don't flatter yourself."

"Not flattery. Honesty. Forced proximity is tough under any circumstances. Throw in adrenaline and attraction, and the stakes go up."

"It's going to take more than a good body and a game of poker to get my attention." The change of crises, from identity to desire, was not what she considered an improvement.

"Even if it is one-sided, which I don't believe for a second, the tension is there, and it's draining."

She wasn't about to admit to him, or herself, how close he came to the truth. "Is this where you suggest we have sex?"

From the corner of her eye, she could see him turn in his seat and study her.

"Tempting." His voice deepened, taking on a husky quality.

"I just bet it is." Heat crept up her neck. An unwanted ache pushed closer to full-blown hunger. The confines of the car and the night surrounding them heightened the intimacy of the conversation. "A one-night stand, get it out of our systems, then get on with business. That'd do the trick, right?"

"Except there are two—no, three—major flaws with that theory."

"Oh?" She risked a glance at him.

He straightened in his seat and she caught a glimpse of him tugging on his pant leg as though trying loosen a snug fit. Her suddenly dry throat tightened.

"Flaw number one—" his voice wrapped around her

in the dark "—you're not the one-night stand type. Flaw number two, neither am I."

Silence settled as she waited for him to continue. When it became clear he wasn't going to say any more, she prompted, "I thought you said there were three flaws."

"You can't guess?"

"Enlighten me."

"Flaw number three." He stroked her arm with the back of his hand. "When we make love, it's going to take a lot more than one night, a whole lot more, before I ever get you out of my system."

There weren't enough names for all the emotions that statement brought to life. Longing shivered over her nerves. Understanding followed.

If they made love, she'd never get him out of her system.

Miles of road later, the trees thinned and a sign heralded their approach to a small town. Frank sat up straighter as the car slowed down. He glanced at Elf.

"We're getting low on gas," she explained.

They pulled into the brightly lit gas station and got out of the car. He grabbed the squeegee and cleaned some of the bug splats off the windshield and headlights, as Elf took care of filling the gas tank.

Across the road, a no-name motel sign glowed Vacancy into the darkness. He looked at his watch. Three-thirty in the morning. He looked at Elf, trying to gauge what her reaction might be.

She frowned back at him. "Not a chance, Cabrini."

"Wouldn't dream of suggesting it, Donovan." He purposely used her last name, putting their banter on a lighter, buddy-buddy level. Not that he'd ever had a buddy who looked as good in a miniskirt as she did.

He followed her into the store and used the rest room as she wandered around with a shopping basket over her arm. While she took her turn in the facility, he added some fresh fruit and bottled water to their supplies.

The next aisle brought him face-to-face with a reality check. As he contemplated the variety of "personal health" products, he knew he wanted to make love with Elf. The hunger had been growing from the second he'd looked at her over the barrel of her gun.

He'd read the desire in her eyes, as well.

That there were secrets between them didn't sit well. He knew too little about Angela Donovan to trust her. But Elf had wormed her way under his skin.

One last item went into the basket. Whether it would prove to be wishful thinking or preparedness didn't matter.

"Didja find what you were looking for?" The middle-aged guy behind the counter winked at him.

Frank ignored him, pulled a couple twenties from his pocket and paid for their purchases.

Elf appeared beside him looking slightly fresher, with her face scrubbed clean of any makeup. The shadows beneath her eyes neared epic proportions. She needed to get some rest before total meltdown became a reality.

"Don't bother arguing," he said when she saw the bag in his arms. He held the door for her and shepherded her to the passenger side of the car. He opened Rusty's door. "The police scanner sounds just as good from the passenger seat as the driver's." He held his hand out for the keys.

Light reflected off the Mustang logo on the keychain as she dropped it into his outstretched palm. She didn't say anything, just sank into the passenger seat. The lack of protest proved her level of exhaustion.

He closed her door and trotted around to the driver's side. The grocery bag went into the back seat, and he levered himself behind the steering wheel. The fit was slightly tighter than the passenger side had been, but he could function without too much difficulty. He took his time getting settled and adjusting the mirrors to his liking.

The engine purred to life and he pulled onto the road, continuing in the direction they'd been going. Appreciation for the engine's fine-tuned power grew as he brought the car up to cruising speed.

Elf broke her silence. "Ever hit a deer, Cabrini?"

"No. There weren't too many running around the streets of Boston."

"Well, there are plenty of them running around these woods."

He eased his foot off the gas pedal a little.

"Consider this a test, Cabrini. Anything happens to this car, and you're dead meat."

"Yes, ma'am."

"Watch out for the deer."

He slowed a little more. "How far to the next town?"

"I'm not sure." A yawn muffled her answer. "Should've gotten a map back there."

"We're going to have to stop sooner or later. We need to get some sleep."

"Later." She rested her head on the seat back. "When we get farther away."

He didn't push the issue. She was already half-asleep.

A few miles later the road intersected with another and he headed east. An hour later, she was sound asleep.

As the sun edged over the horizon, turning the expanse of Lake Superior into molten silver, he pulled into a motel parking lot on the edge of Silver Bay.

Elf never stirred when he cradled her in his arms and carried her to a room.

Chapter 9

Light crept through a gap in the motel curtains. Frank heard a tapping and the faint call of "Housekeeping," as the maid entered a room several doors down from theirs.

Elf slept on, as she had since he'd laid her on the bed. He'd slept some, as well, until the warmth of her pressed against his side drew him back to consciousness.

Now he cradled her in front of him and contemplated how the hell he'd managed to get into this fix.

He'd learned his lesson, the hard way, about women who pretended to be something they weren't. All it had taken was one almost-fiancée learning the family fortune was inaccessible.

His parents had warned him—and he had firsthand experience—of false friendships with those who only saw dollar signs when looking at him. He'd had enough of the sycophants and, after college graduation, he'd made a point of keeping a low profile.

He lived off his ATF wages and led a simple life. Then he met her, the woman he believed would be the perfect partner for him. They had common interests and valued the same things in life. At least he'd thought they did.

The weekend he'd planned on proposing, he began with the confession of what he believed to be his deepest secret—family wealth. Right up to the moment he mentioned the family-mandated prenuptial agreement, he thought she'd loved him for the person he was. But it had all been a sham.

She had a revelation of her own—she'd known all along. And while she'd been willing to humor his charade of being an average Joe while courting, she'd had enough of the lifestyle.

It had been a difficult life lesson, but a good one. Except, if he'd learned it as well as he'd thought, how had he gotten tangled up with a woman who made her living by wearing disguises? Sleep hadn't helped him come up with an answer.

He knew the instant she woke. She didn't move, her breathing didn't change, but there was a subtle shift in her body. A renewed tension simmered just beneath the surface as she lay curled against him.

He raised up on one elbow and leaned over to look at her face. "I'd like to think I passed the test."

Her eyes popped open.

"Good morning." He tugged on a lock of her hair. "Do you always wake up fast?"

"What are you talking about? Where are we?" She scrambled off the bed.

"I believe the sign said 'Silver Bay.'"

Relief washed over her face as she realized they were both fully clothed.

She checked her watch. "Noon?"

"That sounds about right."

"Why did you stop?"

"Because you threatened my life if anything happened to that bucket of rust you call a car." He pushed into a sitting position and leaned against the headboard. "I was getting tired, you were already asleep. Stopping seemed like the wisest thing to do, under the circumstances."

"You should have woken me." She paced the narrow path between the door and the sink.

He shook his head. "There was no waking you, Elf."

"You should have tried."

"I pried you out of the car and carried you in here. If that didn't wake you, do you really think you were in any condition to drive?" He took a deep breath. Reasoning with her would be more productive than venting frustration. "When it started getting light, I figured we were better off someplace where we could melt into a crowd."

"Silver Bay isn't exactly a big city."

"No, but ours is just one of a dozen cars in the parking lot."

"We could have kept going."

"Go where? We'd probably have been stopped because we were the only car on the road."

He caught her hand as she walked by him. "Use your brains. Driving aimlessly through the north woods wasn't getting us anywhere." He tugged her down beside him on the bed. "You know I'm right. We need a plan."

"I suppose you have one all worked out."

"Just the first part."

"Which is?"

"Breakfast. We both need caffeine." And he needed to get them away from the bed.

"That's the plan?"

"We gotta start somewhere, Elf. Food seems to be as good a place as any. We can figure out the next step while we eat, then hit the stores for wardrobe and any other supplies we need."

"Wardrobe?"

"Unless you've got a few more things in my size stashed in Rusty's trunk."

"No." She groaned. "Fine. We get something to eat, then we're back on the road."

Angel pushed her plate off to the side. She couldn't stomach one more bite of industrial scrambled eggs. "We need to seriously change your appearance."

"What's wrong with the way I look?"

"A small matter of notoriety." She tapped the newspaper they'd picked up on their way into the restaurant. Prominent on page one of the *Duluth Superior Times* was a police artist's sketch of Frank Cabrini. The "suspected arsonist" caption added to the sense of menace captured in the drawing.

Not for the first time, she thanked her foresight in slapping nerd glasses and a seed company cap on his head when they left the hotel. Without them, the newspaper image came too close for comfort.

Her disguise was less obvious, but equally effective. The skimpy tank top and short skirt she wore provided enough distraction that anyone looking at her wouldn't be thinking about the description of the suspect's "companion."

Cabrini sipped his coffee. "Interesting how close they came to our exact vitals. How do you suppose they did that?"

She'd been struggling with that question since hearing their descriptions broadcast on the ATL. Every time she tried to reason it through she ran into a dead end. "Right now, I'm more interested in how I'm going to fix you."

He studied her with narrowed eyes, then emptied his coffee cup. "What do you suggest?"

"Nothing drastic. Haircut, beard trim. Maybe, if you can tolerate contacts, a change of eye color." She stopped and turned the paper over as the waitress approached the table.

"Can I get you folks anything else?" The waitress stared at Frank. "More coffee?"

"No." He smiled and winked. "Just the check."

"Sure thing." She smiled back.

"We need to leave." Angel leaned across the table and spoke in a low tone. "We've been here too long. She's trying to figure out why you look familiar, and it's only a matter of time before someone leaves their copy of the *Times* lying face up for her to figure it out."

"You don't have to convince me. The back of my neck's been itching since we sat down." He slid out of the red vinyl booth and met the waitress at the cash register.

Angel studied the other patrons as he settled the bill.

Most of them looked like the typical small-town diner habitués. The only one who caused any real concern was the town cop. He stood next to the register with a to-go cup of coffee in his hand as Cabrini paid the bill.

Her stomach did a slow flip as the cop said something to him. She held her breath, waiting to see if recognition would dawn. *Come on, come on. Quit acting like he's your new best buddy.*

Cabrini finally turned and headed back to where she stood. The cop watched him, and Angel watched the cop. She didn't protest when Cabrini slid his arm around her waist. They strolled out the door and down the street to the car.

As soon as they were out of sight of the diner, she tried to pull away, but he clamped his arm tighter.

"Uh-uh, Elf. He's going to be watching us all the way, so play nice."

"What the Halifax were you doing back there? You couldn't just pay the bill and leave?"

"Not when there was information to be had."

"Like what?"

"Like the fact that the local law enforcement offices just received updated info on the suspected arsonist team working its way through the vicinity."

"Team?"

"Reports are they started with a fancy cabin over on Quay Lake, and were last seen headed north." He stopped beside Rusty and held the door open for her. "Our friendly officer was just heading over to the station to pick up some flyers with the artist's sketch of the big bad firebug and his accomplice."

"Accomplice?" She slapped the key ring in his outstretched hand and got in the car.

"Yeah. Seems he's working with a woman." He closed the door before she could respond.

Real fear had her regretting every bite she'd just eaten.

Cabrini climbed behind the wheel and started the engine.

"Dumb and careless, Cabrini. Dumb and careless."

"What?" He pulled away from the curb and headed out of town.

"That's who the cops catch. The dumb ones and the careless ones."

"We're in good shape then, because we're neither."

"Oh, really? What do you call having a friendly little chat with the local cop? Do you think he didn't get a good look at your face? After he picks up those flyers, how long do you think it'll be before he makes the connection?"

"Long enough for you to work your magic." He pinned her with a steady look. "I'm trusting you to do as good a job transforming me as you do with yourself and this car. Think you're up to it?"

He trusted her? What kind of an idiot was he? She'd done nothing to merit his trust. If he thought for one second that she'd make some sort of sacrifice for him, he had woefully misjudged her. The only person she sacrificed for was her mother. The sooner he realized it, the safer she'd be.

Safer?

Where had that come from? Time enough to worry about that later.

Right now, Cabrini needed a dose of reality. "What makes you so sure I won't call the cops myself and turn you in?"

"Because you know the truth. You just don't want to admit it."

"What truth would that be?"

"That good old Dex set both of us up, and it's going to take both of us to figure out why."

"I don't need you to help figure out anything."

"I think you do. Otherwise you'd see the connection. Who else knows our descriptions?"

"Anyone with access to the DMV records."

"Who else knows we're together?"

Damn him. "You're wrong."

"Why are you protecting him?"

"I'm not."

"Why won't you tell me who he is?"

"You already know. Dex is an old—"

"Family friend," he interrupted. "Yes, I know that. What I don't know is why he hired you to get me out of town. Why did he set us up to be killed?"

"He didn't."

"You sure about that?"

"He isn't trying to kill us." Her jaw ached from clenching it so tight.

"You've got to trust me, Elf. That's the only way we're going to make it through this alive."

"Trust you? Like you trust me? Does that mean you're going to tell me your client's name?"

Angel's ringing cell phone interrupted Cabrini's silence. She flipped it open, thankful for the distraction. "Donovan."

"Angela," her mother's voice came through the phone. "I need to talk to you."

"Mom?" Fear iced over her anger at Cabrini. Her mother rarely called. Getting a second call from her in less than twenty-four hours kicked up all sorts of fears. "What's happened?"

She ignored Cabrini's inquisitive look. She'd rather handle this someplace where he wouldn't be listening to every word she said, but that was impossible, given they were trapped in a small car. She shifted in her seat, turning slightly away from him.

"You need to come home, Angela. As soon as you can."

She sat up straight at her mother's tone. She sounded different, more alert than she had in years. "What's going on? Where's Corie?"

"She's outside. I don't have much time before she comes back. You need to come home. It's very important."

"Can you tell me why, Mom?"

"It would be better done in person. I need to give you something."

"I'll be done with this job in a couple days and we'll have all the time we need then."

"No, it's starting again. You have to come home

now." The urgency in her mother's voice set off alarms. "The fire—just come home."

What was starting again? Was she talking about the cabin fire?

In the background noise of the phone, the doorbell chimed. "Come home, Angela. It's time you learned the truth."

The connection went dead. She looked at the phone, trying to understand what had just happened. Her mother had sounded upset but…normal.

"Is everything all right?" Cabrini's question broke into her thoughts, bringing her back to their current surroundings. They were approaching a highway overpass.

"We need to go south."

"Where?"

"Back to the Cities."

"I thought we'd established that wasn't a good idea."

"That was before your mug got plastered all over the newspapers up here. Now, every small-town cop with delusions of grandeur is going to be dreaming of being The Man who brings you down."

"Good point." He took the entrance ramp onto the highway. "South it is."

"We need to get you out of those clothes."

"I'm flattered, Elf." He looked straight ahead, but a smile pulled up the corner of his beard.

"Get over it, Cabrini. We still need to do something about your appearance."

"Are you sure that's what you meant?"

She chose to ignore him. "We'll detour over to St. Cloud, pick up what we need to perform your transformation."

Several miles passed before Cabrini spoke again. "Are you going to tell me what that call was about?"

"No."

"Why not?"

"Because it has nothing to do with you."

"Maybe not, but it upset you. Maybe you could use a friend to talk it out with."

"And you're proposing that you're the friend?"

"You have to admit, we've gotten to know each other pretty well."

The idea tempted her. The more time they spent together, the more she realized how alike they were. "I don't think so."

"What are you afraid of?"

She shook her head. No way was he going to lure her into that conversation. The last thing she needed was him acting as her shrink.

"Okay, then. I'll guess the conversation and you can tell me how wrong I am."

She snorted.

"You were talking to your mother. She wants you home. She's worried about you. You're worried about her."

"I'd be impressed if all that weren't so obvious as to be meaningless."

"What do you mean?"

She ticked off each item. "One, I started my conversation with 'Mom,' so no mystery there. Two, universal truth—mothers worry about their children, so it's an easy guess that she's worried about me and wants me home, where she'd know that I'm okay. Three, I told you yesterday that Mom is fragile. The logical assumption from that is that I'm worried about her." She shook her head. "So much for your stellar observational techniques."

"You have to admit, I'm a good listener."

"Give it up, Cabrini."

A few miles later, he broke the silence. "What do you have in mind for my disguise?"

Finally, a safe topic, one she could get her hands around without much risk. "Nothing too drastic. We can accomplish quite a bit with clothes. We'll have to hit a couple stores." She glanced at her watch and groaned. "That's going to be a problem."

"You don't like shopping?"

"The problem is it's Sunday. The mall will be closed by the time we get to St. Cloud." She kneaded her fingers through her hair. "We can still hit the discount stores and get the basic necessities to start, but the bulk of it will have to wait until tomorrow morning. You're proving to be a very expensive assignment, you know that?"

"I'm not sure I follow."

"I already laid out a pile of money for your clothes which are now ashes."

"We could go to my room in Minneapolis."

"Too risky, don't you think?"

"Probably."

"Besides, we should get your new look in place before we venture back to the Cities."

"What you really mean is that we're going to spend a night together in a motel, aren't we?"

Memory of waking that morning sent threads of electricity curling through her stomach. She'd been snuggled against his warmth, his arm draped over her waist, holding her close. The unusual sensations of comfort and safety seemed at odds with waking in the arms of a man. And yet, that was exactly what her first thought had been.

The men she met in her line of work were criminals. The men her friends introduced her to fell into two categories—suits and uniforms. She lost interest in the suits when they could find no common ground. The uniforms lost interest in her when they realized how much they had in common, and how unimpressed she was with their stories.

Cabrini was different, beyond her realm of experience. They were equals. They respected each other, even through the frustration of their impasse.

Chances of meeting someone like him didn't bear calculation.

Spending an entire night with him could open a world of possibility that she'd like to explore.

Reality intruded. She couldn't risk a night confined in a room with Frank Cabrini.

But there was little help for it. She'd just have to keep busy with transforming him from scruffy day laborer to yuppie office worker.

Frank settled low into the passenger seat as Elf pulled out of the discount store parking lot. "I've got a bad feeling."

She checked her rearview mirror and changed lanes. "Me, too. That security guard seemed overly diligent."

"Yeah, I'd say it was a bit odd to search our bags while letting that home stereo system walk out the door without a second glance."

"We need to get off— Aw, Shakopee."

"What?" He started to turn around but stopped when she clamped her hand around his arm.

"Cop car on our tail. And there go his lights." She slowed and pulled to the side of the road. "Maybe he'll…" She closed her eyes and wrung the steering wheel. "He's stopping. Cover your face. You're drunk and sound asleep, got it?"

He slumped a little lower in his seat, and the ball cap slid down to shade his face. From the corner of his eye, he watched in amazement as she shimmied out of her seat. The process shortened her skirt from mini to barely there. The length of bare leg she flashed guaranteed distraction of any straight male within a ten-mile radius.

He needed some cool air and wished he could open the window. All he could do was pray.

"Officer?" Elf's voice held just the right amount of confusion and innocence. "Is there a problem? I wasn't speeding, was I?"

"No, ma'am." Gravel crunched on the passenger side.

Frank let his head loll to one side and did his best impression of a drunken snore. From beneath the hat bill, he could just make out Elf's shape, framed in the open car door. The image had his heart pumping just a little heavier.

"Did I miss a stop sign?"

"No, ma'am." The cop's voice, and footsteps, moved from the passenger side.

"I had my seat belt fastened." Elf continued, naming possible infractions, pausing for each answer.

Frank's admiration grew. By the time the cop got to the driver's side, she had effectively eliminated nearly every possible reason for a legal stop.

She knew it, too. "I don't understand, Officer…Novak. Why did you stop us?"

"The fuzzy dice, ma'am. You shouldn't have anything like that hanging from your rearview mirror."

"I'm sorry. They were a gift from a friend who passed away. I guess sentiment overruled sense."

"I understand. We've been ordered to crack down on the little things. Zero tolerance and all that. Besides, there's a report of an arsonist on the run in the area, so we need to be extra cautious."

"You thought we might be him?"

"Just a precaution. I'm sure you understand. Is your passenger all right?"

"My brother?" She turned and bent over to look in at him. The pose must have given the cop an eyeful because he began to cough. "He'll be fine. He just had too much weekend and too little sense." She chuckled, the sound low and sexy, as she straightened and turned around. "That ever happen to you?"

"Yes, ma'am. I mean, no. Ma'am." The cop's voice faded as he beat a retreat to his cruiser. "You can go. Sorry for the inconvenience."

"No problem, Officer Novak. You're just doing your job." The cop drove away and she sank back into the driver's seat. "Cresco, that was too close."

"You did well." His next words stuck in his throat when she turned toward him.

A blush darkened her cheeks, and she tugged on her skirt hem as she settled in her seat. "Let's get out of here and find someplace safe for the night."

Safe? He wasn't sure such a thing existed. Not for them.

A few miles out of town, Elf stopped at a motel advertising free cable TV. "I'll get a room away from the road."

While she used their dwindling cash reserves and checked them in, he parked the car at the rear of the building.

A room. This time they'd both be conscious. The possibility of what the night might hold warmed his blood. When she waved to him from the back entrance, he gathered their purchases and trotted over.

Supper consisted of pizza and soda, delivered to the room, eaten in silence while they watched the news. No mention of arson or a manhunt for suspects helped them shake off a little of the tension.

They got to work on his appearance. Elf started with his hair. Laying a bath towel over his shoulders, she set about trimming the ragged length.

He sat, silent, acutely aware of her nearness. Her soft vanilla scent surrounded him, enticing him with memories of her asleep in his arms.

She stepped back and studied him with a critical eye. He sighed with relief at the reprieve.

It was short-lived. She started on his beard.

She made a couple of cuts, then stepped back, frowning. "This isn't working. I'm at the wrong angle." She knelt in front of him and leaned in close.

His body reacted with record speed at the brush of her torso against his inner thigh. He caught his breath.

Her eyes widened and she scrambled away. "Uh, no. Not that, either."

She looked around the room and pointed at the small table. "Maybe if you stand there."

They finally got themselves arranged in a workable configuration, and she began grooming his beard.

The process was sweet torture. He enjoyed her nearness, breathing in her scent and losing himself in the sensations of her touch.

She seemed oblivious to the effect she had on him. All of her concentration focused on her task. She finished with a few last snips and a nod of approval. "Much better."

"You think so?" He took the scissors and comb from her hands and laid them on the table behind him.

She folded the towel and used it to brush stray hairs off his shoulders. "Definitely more civilized."

"And that's better?" He caught her by the hips, holding her in place between his legs. Leaning forward, he brushed her cheek with his newly trimmed beard.

Her lips parted on a little gasp.

She'd left enough length that his whiskers were a soft, dense pad that telegraphed every sensation straight to his belly.

Where else could he touch her, and what would her reactions be? He nuzzled her neck, just below her ear. She shivered.

She rested her hands on his waist, her fingers kneading as though she couldn't decide whether to push him away or pull him close.

He knew exactly what he wanted to do. He slid one arm around her waist and pulled her closer, cupping the back of her head in his hand as he captured her lips in a devouring kiss.

This was what he'd been hungry for, ever since the first one. That time, he'd been handcuffed. The second time, the cabin had exploded. This time, he didn't plan on stopping until there were explosions of another sort.

She slid one arm around his waist, the other around his shoulder, threading her fingers into his hair. Her rapid breath tickled through his beard, lending another erotic sensation to the experience.

They fit together perfectly.

He scooped her into his arms and carried her to the bed. Laying her in the center, he stretched out beside her. He slipped his hand beneath the hem of her T-shirt and traced idle patterns across her belly, tickling her navel with his little finger.

Every breath she took trembled. He brushed a soft kiss across her cheek and whispered, "I'll admit I was glad the nose ring was fake."

Trailing kisses, he eased down her length until he was level with her belly. He laid a kiss next to her unpierced navel. "But I am disappointed this wasn't real." He kissed her again, dipping his tongue in, tasting her.

Her breath left on a shuddering sigh.

He liked having that effect on her and didn't try to hide his satisfied smile.

She weaved her fingers through his hair and tugged, drawing him back so she could kiss him. He let her have her way, enjoying her fumbling as she pulled his shirt free of his jeans.

Each touch, each taste, each sigh, fed the next. He lost track of who led, who followed. All that mattered was the pleasure, the satisfaction of connecting with this woman on the most elemental level.

When the last of their clothes fell to the floor, he stroked her naked length, aching at her beauty.

She pulled him close and kissed him with a desperate hunger that matched his.

The scent of vanilla and heat and desire wrapped around them. He rolled, pulling her with him. She slid over his chest, leaving trails of electricity in her wake.

Her leg brushed across his hip and she straddled him. *So close.* He held his breath, watching her, waiting for her next move.

She closed her eyes and traced her fingers from his collarbone to his hips and back. Each caress, a sweet torture. She was killing him with her touch.

His pulse kept time with his breath. He mimicked her motions, trailing caresses over her back. Shivers chased after his hands.

He pulled her close, starved for another kiss. As their lips met and tongues danced, he held her and rolled again.

With their positions reversed, he pushed into her, going slow, savoring every millimeter. They'd been working toward this for so long, now that he was finally inside her, he was going to make it last forever. Or at least until he was all the way home.

Holy heaven, she was tight. He pushed a little deeper

and her muscles clenched around him, nearly sending him over the edge. Not yet, not yet. A little deeper, and a barrier released. He settled all the way in and held still, feeling her pulse surround him, savoring the sensations as they rolled over his skin.

He began to pull out and repeat the whole sweet process again. The going was much easier. He froze in place. She still tensed, her fingers digging into his shoulders. He reared back to look her in the face. The position pushed him deeper inside her, and she winced.

Sweet God, no. He searched her face, hoping to see the denial to the question he had to ask. "You're a virgin?"

A convulsive swallow was her only answer.

One more thing he should have known about her, but hadn't. How many other secrets did she have, and how had he gotten caught in her trap?

He understood, then, so many things, and none of them changed the single fact crashing around in his brain. He was her first. She'd been a virgin.

"Oh, Elf. You should have told me."

"Would it have made any difference?"

His throat ached at the fear he heard in her small voice.

Her first time.

"Not with the outcome. Just with how we got there."

"I didn't think you'd be able to tell. I'm sorry."

He brushed her hair back with a hand that trembled. "I'm not. I just wish…"

"I'm sorry. If you tell me what you like…" Her voice trailed off.

He chuckled, and her eyes widened as he moved deep inside her.

Did she really think he'd reject her? Or that he'd be disappointed?

Fear of his own built. What if he screwed up? Disappointed her? The responsibility of initiating her nearly paralyzed him. He had to do this right. She needed to enjoy this or it would shadow her experience with every future partner.

Screw that. There weren't going to be any other partners. Not for her, not for him.

He needed her to enjoy this for herself. For the two of them.

For the future he wanted with her.

"There will be plenty of time for you to learn what I like. Right now, we're going to focus on what you like." He began to pull out, and she wrapped her legs around him, keeping him in place, pulling him back. Her eyes glazed over as the sensations took control.

"Guess that works." He shifted, and her breath caught. "And that."

He kissed her, and her muscles tightened around him. Or maybe he grew harder. He couldn't distinguish anymore which was which. He just knew he had to move or he was going to die. "I'm sorry, Elf. It's the basics this time. Or I might not live to give you a second time."

"You lead. I'll follow."

He tried to keep the pace slow, give her time to adapt, but instinct drove him, and she did follow him. All too soon, he reached the limit of his control. His body pulsed with release.

As he collapsed, he pulled her close, sheltering her in his arms. "Next time will be better, Elf. I promise."

And what of the promise he'd made to himself? Would he ever know the real woman beneath all the disguises?

Chapter 10

Angel tried to pull away from Cabrini, but he rolled onto his back, pulling her with him and winding the sheets around them, binding them together. Her heart, lodged in her throat, still pounded in the aftermath of making love.

He tightened his hold, sweeping one hand down the length of her back. "Stay, just for a bit." He kissed her forehead. "We need to talk."

"Good idea. We need to get a strategy figured out for tomorrow. First thi—" Her words ended in a squeak as he rolled again, this time ending back on top of her.

"Uh-uh. Tomorrow can wait. We need to talk about what just happened."

As a topic of conversation, "what just happened" resided at the very bottom of her list. "Is that really necessary?"

"You don't think so?"

"I thought guys don't normally like the touchy-feely stuff afterwards."

"Very few of our interactions can be called normal." He brushed the hair off her forehead with a gentle hand. "Why, Elf? You've waited so long. Why now? Why me?"

She shrugged and avoided looking him in the eyes. "It seemed like as good a time as any."

All signs of warmth and tenderness left his face. He rolled off her and out of the bed. Three steps away, he stopped. The soft room light cast a golden sheen across his back.

She sat up, pulling the sheets around her in a cocoon. When he pivoted slowly to face her, her stomach clenched.

Worry merged with an uneasy awareness. She'd been right—there would be no getting him out of her system.

He stood in front of her in all his naked glory. All of it. Every square inch. Naked.

He had a beautiful body. She tried to be casual, to keep from revealing just how much of an effect he had on her. Denying it altogether would be much easier, if he'd put some clothes on.

Instead, he seemed determined to stand in the middle of the room, buck naked and talking. A moment of relief came as he scooped their clothes from the floor and sorted his from hers. The buzz of his words began to take shape and meaning as he jerked on his boxers and jeans.

Her tank top and skirt landed on the bed next to her. She made no move to pick them up. "Whoa. Rewind, Cabrini. What are you talking about?"

He shook his head and slumped into the room's only chair. "We skipped a couple important topics of conversation, things we should have covered before…"

He leaned forward, resting his elbows on his knees, steepling his hands in front of his mouth. "I'm in good health, meaning no STDs. I'm guessing the same holds true for you. Nonetheless, that's no excuse not to practice safe sex. Which we didn't."

Understanding began to spread like an unwelcome dawn.

"Is there any chance you're on the Pill?"

"No." She shot off the bed as his full meaning registered. *Safe sex. Birth control. No protection.* Under cover of her bedsheet toga, her hand stole to her stomach.

"I really screwed up." He leaned back again and crossed his arms.

"You weren't exactly acting alone, Cabrini."

"True, but that doesn't excuse my carelessness. I should have known better."

"Don't get your boxers in a bunch just yet." She dug her fingers through her hair. "We're okay. I think. I need a calendar." She glanced at him and he shook his head.

"It'll be okay," she muttered as she grabbed her clothes and headed for the bathroom. The litany became a prayer as she showered.

Coherent thought skittered into dismay every time she tried to focus. She'd trailed Cabrini for weeks but had only started to get to know the man behind the rough exterior.

His questions rang in her ears. *Why now? Why me?* She didn't have any good answers. Only questions of her own.

Why had she said yes after knowing the man for barely two days. She was too practical to confuse their nascent partnership with affection. And she certainly couldn't think it was the beginnings of love.

Since her father's murder, she'd cultivated a protective shell around her heart. It had been her protection from suffering her mother's fate. How had Cabrini worked his way through her defenses?

How could she have left herself so vulnerable when the one thing she knew for sure was that he would leave and, like her mother, she'd be alone.

If it turned out she'd gotten pregnant... *I'll always have a part of him.*

The echo of that idea drove her from the bathroom.

Cabrini still sat at the table. "Elf, whichever way it works, we'll be okay."

Okay? By what definition?

He pushed a piece of paper toward her. He'd sketched out a calendar of June and July.

She counted days and looked at him. "No worries. We're safe." And the disappointment hurt more than she'd ever admit.

The next morning, they went shopping for Frank's disguise at the first suburban mall on the road into the Twin Cities metro area. Dress shirts, polo shirts, a blazer, pants and shoes. The total the sales clerk announced had Elf sucking in a breath.

"Chill out." He shouldered her out of the way. "My clothes, my cash."

"Fine by me." She turned away and made a call on her cell phone to someone she addressed as "Grampa Fred." The list of what he didn't know about her kept growing.

As they drove through the outer suburbs, she made another call. "Hi, Corie. I'm going to be stopping in for a little while and need a favor."

Frank listened to her side of the conversation until, plans evidently in place, she pocketed the phone.

"Care to fill me in on the details?" he asked.

"We're stopping by my mother's. I need to pick up some things."

"That's all?"

Her hands tightened on the steering wheel, turning her knuckles white. "That's all that concerns you."

"I'm concerned someone could be waiting for us."

"According to the neighborhood watchdog, all's quiet on the home front."

He let that sit until she backed into the empty two-car garage of a house on a quiet street. "Will I get to meet your mother?"

"I'm not sure that's wise."

"Why not?"

"Meeting new people is hard for her. She's had enough stress these past couple days. I'd rather not add to it."

"So, what? I stay in the garage?"

"I wouldn't do that to you, Cabrini. You can come down to the basement. We can pull a few more accessories for you from my supply. As long as you stay downstairs, you're more than welcome in my mother's home."

He chuckled. "Mothers often try to keep me in the basement. I think it's some fear that I'm not housebroken."

She ignored his little joke. Shoving the suitcase they'd picked up into his hands, she hefted a duffel bag out of the car trunk and led the way downstairs.

They entered a large room, probably intended to be the family's rec room, currently housing a home office. Shelves lined one wall, holding an amazing array of wig forms, hats, glasses and other props. Several rolling racks, each covered with a large dust sheet, lined another wall.

A small vanity butted against a large makeup mirror suitable for any backstage dressing room. The lights flickered to life at the touch of a switch, and she pointed to the chair.

"Let's see what we can do about your eyes."

He sat, and she pulled a drawer open. "Have you ever worn contacts?"

"Yes."

"Then this shouldn't be too difficult. Try these." She handed him a pair of disposable colored lenses.

It took a couple of tries, but he finally had the lenses in and could keep his eyes open.

Elf nodded in approval. "Good. Put these on." She handed him a pair of steel wire-rimmed glasses. "For the professorial look."

He slipped them on and studied his new image reflected in the makeup mirror. Neatly trimmed hair and beard, brown eyes, glasses—a stranger stared back at him. "I had my doubts, but you do know your stuff."

She handed him some of his new clothes, the tags removed. Pointing to a door, she said, "You can change in there."

The room she'd indicated was actually a bathroom. As he peeled his borrowed T-shirt over his head, he heard footsteps coming down the stairs. He cracked the door open just enough to peek out. A woman came into view.

"Angela?" her soft voice barely reached him.

"Mom?" Surprise colored Elf's voice. "What are you doing down here?"

"We only have a few minutes." Maryam Donovan glanced up stairs. "She'll be back soon."

"Corie? Of course she'll be back. She just ran an errand for me."

"I can't talk to you with her around. Not really, not about what matters."

"Mom, I don't understand. What are you talking about?"

"I'm much better now. You need to talk to Dr. Brenna. She can explain it all to you, but there's no time for that now."

A frown creased Elf's forehead. Her mother reached up to smooth away the lines.

"Everything will be all right. You'll see. I remembered, sweetie. I finally remember...so much. Nothing is what it seems. That's why it didn't make sense. You have to be careful."

"I will. You know I always am."

"I hired someone. He's going to help you find the truth."

"What do you mean, Mom? Who've you hired?"

Frank tensed, waiting for Maryam to mention The Diamond Group. How would Elf react?

"He'll help you sort everything out."

Overhead, a door closed, and footsteps moved from the kitchen to the living room and back.

Maryam pressed something into her daughter's hand. "This will explain everything. Just remember, he loved us."

Footsteps sounded on the stairs. "Maryam?" another woman's voice called down.

The new arrival came down the stairs. "What are you doing down here?" She looked from mother to daughter. "I'm sorry, Angela. I thought Maryam was napping, and took a little extra time to get the car washed at the gas station."

Frank watched, fascinated as Maryam seemed to shrink into herself.

Elf turned to face the newcomer. "It's okay, Corie. We were having a nice talk, weren't we, Mom?"

She didn't respond. From all appearances, she

seemed to have lost herself in some other world. She looked around the basement room as though she'd never seen it before.

Elf slipped her arm around her mother's shoulders and turned her toward the stairs. "Why don't you go back to the living room. I have to leave in a little bit, but I'll come say goodbye. Okay?"

Maryam nodded and started up the stairs, pausing on each riser, seeming to gather her strength for the next one.

Corie waited until footsteps crossed the floor overhead before turning to Elf. "She's never done that before. She's always stayed upstairs."

"It's all right. She heard me come in and followed me down."

"Did she seem…different?"

"What do you mean?" Elf disappeared from Frank's limited range of vision. He could hear the rasp of suitcase zippers.

"I'm not sure. Since she started seeing Dr. Brenna, sometimes she doesn't seem like herself."

"She hasn't been herself in nearly twenty years." He heard the anger and sadness in Elf's voice. "We need to be patient while the new meds take effect."

"Maybe. I still think you should get a second opinion." Corie shrugged. "Your mom's car is ready to go. When will you be back?"

"I don't know. This case is a bit more complex than I anticipated."

"Anything I can help with?"

"Just…if anyone calls or comes looking for me, you haven't seen me."

Corie looked around the room. "Including Mr. Dexter?"

Frank ducked out of sight as she turned in his direction.

"Anyone."

"I better check on your mom." Corie headed up the stairs.

"Thanks. I'll be up in a bit."

He waited for Corie's footsteps to cross the main floor before he left his hiding place.

"Let's get our things in the car." Elf handed him the suitcase and picked up a smaller carry-on bag. She led the way, waving him into the garage when she was sure the coast was clear.

The trunk of a silver Lexus popped open. He looked from the car to her, and she tossed him a set of keys. She went to say goodbye to her mother while he loaded their supplies in the trunk.

Could her single income really stretch far enough to afford a new luxury car and live-in companion for her mother? She had to be carrying a pretty heavy debt load.

Or be getting help from someone.

Chapter 11

Cabrini maneuvered the luxury car through the midday city traffic. "What's with all the hamster tubes?" He pointed at the enclosed pedestrian walkways over the streets.

"We prefer to call them skyways. Turn left." Angel pointed at the intersection. "Most of downtown Minneapolis is connected by them. You can get from Target Center on one end to the Convention Center on the other end without ever going outside."

"This is a good thing?"

"Very good, considering the local climate. Come wintertime you'll see—" She stopped. No, he wouldn't. Cabrini would be long gone before the first snowfall ever whitened the landscape.

That was fine with her. She didn't need or want him around, complicating her life. The novelty of working with a partner would be long past stale if he was still around in the winter.

Traffic stopped behind a delivery truck. He shifted lanes with a smooth turn of the wheel. "Nice car."

She shrugged and directed him to the Marriott City Center hotel.

"All the money you save by driving the junker, you put into this for your mother?"

His probing hit a tender situation. She didn't really want to explain to someone who wouldn't be around long enough to understand. "It's a gift."

"Quite the gift. What does one do to merit such generosity?"

She shot a quelling look in his direction. "Not much, just lose a spouse in the line of duty." *And lose your mind in grief.*

"I'm not following."

She sighed. "Dex likes to help out when he can. Every couple years, he leases a new car for Mom. She gets to ride around in style whenever Corie or I take her out. And he gets to assuage his guilt for having survived the fire that killed Dad."

"So, he atones by providing you and your mother with a lakeside cabin and a luxury car? And he throws work your way every now and then."

"No."

"And yet, he had you track me down so he could have a 'discussion' with me." He held his hand up, cutting off her protest before she could voice it. "Give it up. Dex is your client. We both know I'm right, so cut the evasion. We'll figure out what's going on a whole lot faster if we're both working with all the available information."

"Fine. Let's start with clearing up your misperception. I rarely take jobs from family or friends. It tends to get complicated."

"What made this different?"

She shrugged, wishing she hadn't taken this assignment. *Complicated* didn't begin to describe the situation. "He never asked before."

"In other words, what you really mean is, you don't take work from friends or family who don't ask?"

"Nooo." She drew out the word as she dug a little deeper into her short supply of patience. "He said he was in a delicate position and needed someone he could trust to discreetly handle a situation."

"Me being the situation."

"As it turns out, yes."

"Hold that thought." He pulled the car into the line for the hotel's valet parking. "We'll continue this when we get to the room."

"Fine." Relief sapped some of the tension from between her shoulders. She reached into the back seat for her duffel bag. The action brought her close enough to Cabrini to catch his scent and send her libido into hyperdrive. *Dangerous ground.* She pushed the car door open. "Check in under your agency name. I'll be back in a couple hours. And Mistah Cabrini, suh?"

He raised one eyebrow at the return of her southern accent. "Yes?"

"Two rooms." She escaped the car and sauntered down the street. Until she assumed her next identity, they made too memorable an odd couple to check in together. Besides, she had things to do.

Starting with a little kickboxing. That would take care of the day's exercise requirement and combine nicely with her need to vent a little frustration.

Frank checked them into adjoining rooms, opened the connecting doors and spent a few minutes unpacking their bags.

He caught himself lingering over the texture and

style of Elf's clothes, trying to picture her in the tailored business suits. The faint scent of vanilla clung to the fabric, and he imagined peeling each layer away to reveal the woman beneath.

Every time he thought he had a handle on the "real" Elf, some new discovery forced him to acknowledge how little he actually knew about her. Self-preservation dictated that he keep that in mind and not get sucked into a relationship doomed to fail.

Memories of the previous night's revelation stirred and ignited a hunger for more.

Self-preservation be damned. If he had any choice in the matter, the second room wouldn't be getting much use.

Once the last of his clothes had been hung in the closet and the luggage stowed, he wandered around the room.

Their location in one of the triangular building's corners provided a wide-angle view of the busy downtown. In contrast, the short hall outside the room seemed eerily quiet.

He checked his watch. Still a stretch of time to kill before Elf's return. He took advantage of her absence to check in with his boss.

"It's about time." Kat greeted him in her typical brusque manner.

"We've been a little busy."

"So have I." She gave him the pertinent information she'd gathered on one Angela Marie Donovan, daughter of Patrick, a Minneapolis police officer killed in the line of duty.

"I already knew most of that. Tell me something I don't know."

"Fine. Let's look at Officer Donovan's former partner. We managed to dig up a little more on him through

the national databases and a few well-placed resources."
The sound of rustling papers came over the phone line.

He settled at the desk and concentrated on the information Kat relayed.

The picture taking shape wasn't pretty, but it certainly solved the mystery of Elf's role. In Marvin Dexter's scheme, she was one more low card, easily
sacrificed on the way to a better deal.

"Frank, be careful." Kat's concern filtered through
his thoughts. "I'm beginning to think it's time to send
some backup."

"Not necessary, boss. I already have a partner. One's
enough."

"You trust Ms. Donovan that much?"

"Yes." More than trust, the realization settled in his
chest with a warm certainty. "The bigger question is,
does she trust me?"

"You better find out. She's facing a difficult decision,
and I don't want you paying for her choice with your
life."

"It won't come to that." He hoped. "I'll check back
with you tomorrow."

Formulating a plan for their next step provided a
good excuse to avoid delving too far into his feelings
for Elf. He leafed through the new information, fitting
the details with the events of the past couple days.

The ringing phone broke into his concentration.

"Where are you?" Elf sounded tired.

He gave her the room numbers. A couple of minutes
later, a firm knock sounded at the door.

When he swung the door open, a stranger stood in
front of him. Simple, black heels and knee-skimming
skirt framed shapely legs. The tailored jacket of the
classic black suit accented a trim waist. Subtle makeup
and dark, rich brown hair, combed in a sleek style, com-

bined to highlight the woman's elegant bone structure. Dark-rimmed glasses didn't disguise her deep blue eyes from him.

He let loose with a low whistle. "You've done it again, Elf."

She brushed past him and dropped her duffel bag in the adjoining room. He trailed after her and watched her unpack. "New wig?"

"No. *My* hair. *My* color. I'm tired of—" She turned to face him. "Did you want something?"

Yeah, I'd like to know what you're tired of. He let her unfinished comment go, for the moment. Other, more pressing, issues needed to be addressed. "Come in here. Let's talk."

"Talk, as in, the equal sharing of information?" She tossed her bag into the closet and slid the door shut. "Or as in, you ask all the questions and I get nothing?"

"You may not like the answers, but you'll get to ask your questions, I promise." He led the way into the larger room.

She sat in one of the low chairs, crossing her legs and flashing him enough thigh to kick his pulse into his throat.

He battled his reaction the only way available to him at the moment—he talked about the case.

"I checked in with my boss and she had some interesting information to share. It seems Marvin Dexter, formerly a Minneapolis police officer partnered with Patrick Donovan—your father—has been busy moving up the political ladder since leaving the force. After a number of years on the city council, he now has a good chance of winning the upcoming mayoral election. State governor seems to be the next step on his agenda."

"And his political aspirations are important because…?" Her reaction revealed mild irritation and little else.

"It's important because Dexter—Dex as you call him—hired you and directed you to, essentially, kidnap me. To your credit, you had no idea that was his intention when you accepted his request. He very deliberately kept you in the dark."

"What makes you so sure about that?"

"You said it yourself, Elf. I believe your exact words were 'last week's sauerkraut.'"

She slid a little deeper into her chair, revealing more leg as her skirt hiked up. "What do you want from me?"

"First off, you can quit trying to distract me with your legs." He could admire her tactic of using her body to elicit certain responses. Any good undercover agent would do the same.

He didn't like her applying that tactic to him. "We'll get a lot further if we quit playing games."

She straightened in her chair, returning her skirt back to its modest length. "Does this mean you're finally going to tell me about your client?"

He nodded. "More than you'll want to know, but it's time you learned the truth."

"Truth is a highly flexible concept."

"Then let's stick to the facts."

Frank sat on the couch across from Elf's chair. He'd known this moment would come. That knowledge didn't make it any easier.

Would she be angry at him for not telling her sooner? Or would she continue to deny the evidence?

Realizing how he felt about her, what he hoped they could have in the future, added to the pressure.

"I'm waiting, Cabrini. Let's hear your facts."

The only way he'd get his answers was if he leveled with her. "You've been doing your own investigation on the side, looking into the circumstances of your father's murder."

She crossed her arms. "What's that got to do with anything?"

"Your digging has stirred up a few things, things the parties involved would just as soon never saw the light of day."

"That's usually the case when something dirty gets buried."

"Twenty years ago, your father started an independent investigation looking into a series of arsons. He was close to breaking the case when he was killed and all his information disappeared."

"How do you know this?" Her eyes narrowed.

The facts of the case should be easy enough to relay. The underlying background, though, had him choosing his words with more care than a normal debriefing would warrant. "The Diamond Group was contracted two months ago to investigate an old arson/murder. You and I were on the same track, headed for the same conclusion. It makes a certain sense to get us together and dispose of us at one time, before we could do too much damage."

Elf pushed out of her chair and paced the room. "You still want me to believe someone is trying to kill me?"

"You were getting too close to the truth."

She stopped in front of him, hands planted on her hips, anger radiating from every pore. "What truth?"

"Marvin Dexter killed your father."

She took a step back from him. "That's ridiculous." She backed away another step. "They were partners, closer than brothers."

"Brothers kill brothers."

"No." She turned away.

"I'm not the only one who thinks so."

"Who else?"

"Our client pointed us in that direction."

"Then he's wrong, whoever he is." Her long strides took her from one end of the room to the other.

"She."

"What?" She stopped and turned to glare at him.

"Our client is a she."

Elf resumed pacing, her back stiff and straight. "Then, she's wrong."

"We don't believe so."

"Why now? It's been twenty years. Why is someone coming forward with this crazy theory after all this time?"

"There are a combination of factors." Long before they'd made love, when he'd first realized who Elf was, he'd known he'd have to deal with this revelation. He needed her to believe him, but doing so meant she had to give up some long-held illusions. "The stakes are higher now."

"Politics again."

"With each new level of office, past indiscretions become bigger liabilities. Some can be glossed over. Others, like murder and arson, are harder to dismiss."

"Your client, is she one of his opponents?"

"No. She's a private citizen."

"You said it was a combination of factors. What else is involved?"

He caught her hand as she brushed past him on another circuit of the room. "Our client is recovering from a long-term…misdiagnosis, actually."

Elf sank into the chair.

"Her original doctor disappeared several months ago. We think he may have been eliminated because of what he knew." Frank continued, laying out the facts, watching the reluctant dawn of understanding in her expression. "Our client's new doctor suspected a misdiagnosis and prescribed different medication. As a result, our client has regained some memories. With her increased coherence has come increased awareness of the danger surrounding her. And her daughter."

"No." Elf wrapped her arms around her waist. "It's paranoia. The right medication alleviates that."

He wanted to pull her into his arms, shelter her from the emotions chasing across her expressive face. "Paranoia doesn't rule out real danger."

"If she's in such danger, how did she contact your agency?"

"Through her doctor's office. Kat didn't take this case on until the doctor thoroughly briefed her on the woman's situation. When she was convinced of the reality, she assigned me to the case."

"What did you think when you met with your client?"

"I haven't, yet. Our communication is still routed through the doctor."

"Are you sure the doctor isn't making this up? It could be some elaborate scheme for publicity or something."

"You don't really think Dr. Brenna would do that, do you?"

"Dr...." Elf pushed out of her chair and crossed to the windows. "No." She whispered the denial.

Frank came behind her and rested his hands on her shoulders. Her muscles were tensed rock hard. He kneaded the tight knots. "I'm sorry Elf. I know it's a lot to believe, most of it on faith."

"It's too much. He loves her."

"What?"

"Dex." She pulled away from him. "He loves my mother."

"He told you this?"

"Never in so many words. But it's always been there,

underneath the surface. Everything he's done for us, for her, over the years. It wasn't just survivor's guilt.

"Now you expect me to believe…? No. How could he destroy my mother like that? How could he come to our home and pretend to be our friend if what you say is true?"

"Because, if the information she's provided is true—and we believe it is—the only other alternative would have been to kill her, as well."

All the color drained from Elf's face. He did enfold her in his arms then, holding her as shivers wracked her body, glad she didn't push him away.

Too soon, she gathered herself and pulled back from him.

"I want to meet with her doctor. I want to know why she never saw fit to tell me." Her voice throbbed with anger.

He nodded. "Do you have the number for her office?"

She retrieved her cell phone and punched in the number from memory. "This doesn't mean I believe everything you've told me."

"Fair enough. We'll take this one hurdle at a time."

Elf walked into the adjacent room. She returned almost immediately. "Dr. Brenna's service picked up the call. She's out of town at a conference until Wednesday."

"We'll get in to see her then."

"She tried to tell me," she whispered.

"What?"

"Mom. She tried, a half dozen times at least, to get me to go with her to an appointment." She fiddled with her cell phone, not looking at him. "I was always too busy or made some excuse."

"You couldn't know. Besides, you had to make a living."

"It was easier to let Corie take her to the appointments." She tugged at her hair, ruffling the smooth style. "I didn't want to deal with her illness."

"Beating yourself up isn't going to change anything now. What matters is that we'll see the doctor on Wednesday."

"What do we do in the meantime?"

"I'm thinking room service."

She finally looked him in the eye. "Is eating your solution to everything?"

"I'm Italian." In his family, that generally sufficed as an excuse.

"Go ahead. I'm not hungry."

He pulled her into his arms. "I know it feels like you just got dumped on. It's a lot to handle. But you aren't in this alone."

"No?"

"No." He brushed his hands across her back, trying to comfort her.

"Part of your client service standards?"

He leaned away enough to get a good look at her. Anger, pain and doubt intermingled with a hint of fear in her eyes. "This stopped being about client service the first time I kissed you."

"Tag, and I'm yours? Is that it?" She pulled out of his arms, squared her shoulders and raised her chin. "Well, guess again, Cabrini. I don't need you to take care of me or to help me or to protect me. I'm a big girl and have been doing all that on my own for a long time."

She crossed the room with long, angry strides. "I don't need you." The door connecting their rooms latched shut with a sharp click.

"Yay for you, Elf," he whispered. "The thing is, I need you."

* * *

Angel shed the business suit, scrubbed her face clean and slipped into bed. The exhaustion she'd been fighting all weekend was going to win this battle. She might as well get comfortable for the surrender.

An hour later, the oblivion of sleep still eluded her. She glared at the ceiling, wide awake, restless. Lonely. She slipped on the plush terry robe provided by the hotel and stood at the window, staring out.

Many stories below, traffic flowed. Pedestrians crossed the street. Everything looked so normal.

Would she ever be able to say that about her life? Ever walk down a street hand-in-hand with her partner laughing, stealing a kiss?

Memory of Cabrini and his kisses, the camaraderie they'd shared over the past three days, taunted her. The independence she'd taken such satisfaction in now seemed hollow and no more real than the partnership budding between them. That had been part of the job for him. She'd been part of the job.

A soft knock on the connecting door pulled her from the window. She padded across the room in her bare feet and opened the door a crack. "What?"

"Room service just delivered. I thought you might come join me."

She shook her head. "I'm really not hungry."

"You don't have to eat. Just...come keep me company."

She raised a questioning eyebrow. "We've been in each other's face for the past seventy-two hours. You expect me to believe you're lonely?"

"Seems odd, I know."

"To say the least."

"Please, will you join me?" The plea in his words

pulled at her deep-buried hope. Maybe she could be more than part of a job for him.

"The sleep thing doesn't seem to be working." She opened the door farther. "I suppose I can be awake in your room just as easily as in mine."

Mouthwatering aromas drew her across the room. The service cart held two place settings and a half dozen covered dishes.

"I got a little carried away when I ordered." Cabrini settled into the desk chair and lifted the first cover. Caesar salad. "If you change your mind about being hungry, feel free to help yourself."

He lifted the second cover and revealed angel hair pasta tossed with broccoli, carrots, peppers and tomatoes.

"I suppose it's all vegetables." She lifted another cover to reveal a small baking dish covered with melted cheese.

"That would be the four cheese and tricolor pasta something-or-other."

Oh, Helsinki. He had to have ordered that especially for her. The image wavered as tears welled up in her eyes.

He reached across the small table and scooped up a forkful. "Not bad, but I've had better."

"Danube, Cabrini. What am I going to do with you?"

"Mangi, as my mother always says. Eat. We can figure out the rest after."

That wouldn't be necessary. She'd already figured out too much. Like how much she would miss him when he left.

Chapter 12

Frank stacked the empty dishes back on the service cart and pushed it into the hall. "I'd hate to see the damage if you ever are hungry."

Elf curled into a corner of the couch. "Okay, fine. I admit it. I had something of an appetite after all."

He sat next to her, pulled her feet into his lap and began rubbing.

After an initial surprised jerk, she relaxed with a little moan.

He chuckled. "Gets 'em every time."

"Do this a lot, do you?"

"Five sisters, remember?"

"Yeah, right." She burrowed her hands into her robe pockets and snuggled a little deeper into the couch. "How long have you known?"

Through the entire meal, they'd managed to avoid talking about anything pertaining to their respective assignments. Recess was over. "That my client is your mother? I first suspected when you told me your name. During our poker game, when you talked about your mother, I knew."

"But you didn't say anything."

"Would it have done any good? You weren't ready to hear the truth about Dexter. You're still fighting the idea."

She didn't deny it. "You could have gotten away almost anytime we were at the cabin."

"Probably."

"But you decided to stick around to see what you could get out of me?" Her expression gave away nothing about her thoughts.

The visual cues weren't necessary. He heard her underlying question and knew nothing less than honesty would satisfy her. "Initially, yes."

She tried to pull away, but he wouldn't let her go. "Then, as we got to know each other, I realized we were stronger together, that we needed each other."

"For the sake of your case."

"No. It goes deeper than that."

"I don't know how—" She looked away from him. "I'm used to working alone. I'm not accustomed to…sharing. Or cooperating."

"Me, neither."

"We're a real match made in heaven."

"We've done all right, so far."

"Where does that leave us?"

"Somewhere on the upside of a steep learning curve. And with a case to solve. Once that's no longer a factor, then we'll figure out what's next."

"Professionally or personally?"

"Either, both. Your choice, Elf." He hoped she'd choose both. "Right now, let's discuss our plan for tomorrow."

"We have a plan?"

"Not yet."

She studied him with narrowed eyes. "You have something in mind, though, don't you?"

He met her steady gaze and nodded.

She sighed. "I suppose you want to go see Dex."

"I considered it."

"And?"

"I decided it wouldn't accomplish much, other than alerting him that we're here in town. He's probably already figured out that we're working together. It might be worth keeping our exact whereabouts under wraps."

A little tension drained from her muscles as he continued massaging, but he was a long way from getting her relaxed. Not that he could blame her. Too much of her world had taken a left turn when he'd revealed his client and her mother were the same person. Forcing her to see Dex's betrayal wasn't helping.

He needed her to trust him, and not just for the sake of the investigation.

"We could go to the bank."

Her words caught him off guard. "What bank?"

She pulled a small, green envelope from her robe pocket and held it out on her palm.

A bank name and downtown address were printed on the face of the envelope. He opened the flap and shook out the contents. A single key fell into his hand.

"Mom passed that to me."

Maybe they were closer to trusting than he'd realized. "A safe-deposit key?"

She nodded. "I think so."

"Any idea what's in it?"

"No. I'm not even sure which bank it's in—there've been so many mergers the last few years. Facilities were combined, new offices built... Chances are pretty good that address doesn't even exist as a bank anymore."

"I guess that gives us the task for tomorrow."

"Finding the right bank won't do us much good without an authorized signature."

The key landed on the triangular glass coffee table with a little "ting." "We'll worry about that when we get there." He resumed rubbing her feet and worked his way up her ankles. She had great ankles.

Several minutes passed in silence as he continued massaging his way to her knees. He'd nearly reached his goal when Elf sat up. "Maybe this won't be so hard."

So much for his magic touch entrancing her. "How do you figure?"

"Maybe we do have an authorized signature."

"We do?" He stopped massaging.

"It was so long ago, I'd forgotten about it." She pulled her feet from his lap and reached for the bank envelope. "There were a million papers, and I couldn't keep track of them all." She turned the envelope over and over. "I know I filled out a signature card for the checking account. There may have been others. Including one for this bank."

"When was this?"

"After Dad's murder. Mom had the lawyers put my name on the bank accounts and a bunch of other stuff." She flicked a glance at him.

"If that's the case, then we're in, no sweat."

She sank back into the couch and returned her feet to his lap. "I'm starting to feel lucky."

"Me, too." He slid his hand around the back of her calf and kneaded.

"Don't think I don't know what you're doing."

"Is it working?" He massaged his way farther up her leg with slow, methodical motions.

"Yes." She sighed. "I'm so easy."

"Elf, there is nothing easy about you."

"Somehow, that doesn't sound good." She stretched her arms over her head.

His chuckle caught in his throat as her bathrobe fell open, revealing more leg. And a cow-and-the-moon print nightshirt.

He broke into laughter.

She opened her eyes and pushed herself up on her elbows. "Your seduction technique could use some work, Cabrini."

"I'm sorry, Elf. I hadn't considered that a tough bounty hunter would wear nursery rhyme pj's."

"Bail bond enforcer."

"Whatever." He traced the outline of one moon strategically positioned over her breast. "Do these glow in the dark, too?"

Laughter danced in her eyes as she laid back onto the couch. "You'll never know unless you turn out the lights."

A floor lamp stood next to her end of the couch. He made good use of the opportunity that presented. Inch by slow inch, he worked his way from her knees to her head, sliding his body over hers. By the time he made it within reach of the lamp, he'd forgotten about turning it off.

Cabrini came out of the bathroom wearing boxers and a contented smile. Water from his morning shower glistened on his skin.

Angel wore a smile of her own as she watched him. He'd promised that her second time would be better than the first, and he'd spent hours throughout the night to make it so.

She'd enjoyed every second of it.

He wandered through the connecting door into her room. "We can get breakfast in the restaurant here, then head over to the bank." He bent down to nibble on her lips just long enough to knock her pulse into her target workout range. "Or we could order room service and relax a little longer."

"I don't believe you have relaxing on your mind."

He winked.

She pushed him away. "As tempting an offer as that may be, it's getting late. I'm nearly dressed, and you should be, too."

"Yes, ma'am." He sighed and wandered back into his room, stopping at the closet to grab pants and a shirt.

"I'll go down and get a table at the restaurant." She gathered up the accessories for her businesswoman disguise.

Her cell phone and wallet slid into the black Coach bag she'd scored at a secondhand store. All black was too somber for her mood, so she opted for the deep lavender side of her reversible suit jacket. Her revolver nestled at her back, hidden by discreet tailoring.

She checked herself in the mirror one last time and ran a hand through her hair, smoothing down an unruly cowlick. The styling and new color, which was actually her natural color, would take some getting used to, but, all in all, the look worked. The image reflected in her mirror would blend in at any of the downtown offices. Satisfied, she headed for the hall door.

The faint clatter of china filtered into her room. The maid, probably. Habit and training had her checking outside through the peephole. What she saw froze her hand above the doorknob.

Two men stood outside the door to Cabrini's room. One pushed the service cart to the side of the hall, then took up a lookout post a couple of feet away. The second guy huddled over the electronic door lock.

Both wore nondescript dark suits. Like her, they'd blend into any business office. Like her, they were armed. She'd caught a glimpse of the lookout's gun, holstered under his arm, as he'd pushed the cart out of their way.

Instinct took over and she tore into Cabrini's room. She motioned for silence before he could say anything.

Grabbing his sport coat, she tossed it to him as she whispered, "We've got company."

He caught the navy blazer and slipped it on. "What's happening?"

"Two men breaking in." She faced the door, watching for the telltale turn of the handle. Her fingers itched to pull her gun, but she didn't want to do that unless absolutely necessary.

Cabrini didn't waste time asking any more questions. He swiped his wallet and room key off the credenza, jammed his feet into his shoes and grabbed her arm as he headed for her room.

The first connecting door was nearly shut when she remembered. "Bank key?"

Cabrini's hissed obscenity answered well enough. She pushed back into the room. The green envelope lay on the coffee table on the far side of the room.

She dashed across the space. *Please, please, please,* her silent litany begged, *don't crack the code. A few seconds. That's all I need.*

The envelope skittered off the table as she grabbed the key. *No time, no time.* She pushed Cabrini's newspaper off the table, burying the envelope in a pile of newsprint.

Her ankle twisted as she spun to make the mad dash back across the room. She bit her lip against the pain.

Cabrini caught her when she stumbled through the door. He steadied her against his side as he pulled the first connecting door shut. "They're in."

She nodded and leaned against the door frame.

"Are you okay?"

She waved off his question as she pressed her ear to the connecting door. The sound came through enough that she could tell they were talking, but not clear enough to make out many words. She relayed what she could hear. "Don't touch...entrances covered...wait here..." Her eyes widened and she looked at Cabrini. "Other room."

He swore.

"Yeah. Let's get out of here."

"Your ankle?"

She slipped off her heels, shoved them into her briefcase and pulled on her running shoes. "I'll be fine. Let's book."

Cabrini checked the hallway and motioned her ahead. He followed, resting his hand on the small of her back, over her gun.

The warmth of his hand combined with the weight of her gun in an odd, calming effect. She released a long breath as they headed down the corridor.

The triangular layout of the hotel put the passenger elevators on the hall farthest from their corner room. She spotted another dark-suited man rounding the corner from the elevators.

"Service stairs," Cabrini whispered.

A vague sense of recognition grew as the distance between them and the new arrival narrowed. Two steps away from their escape, he stopped in front of them. "Hello, Angela. You've changed. Again."

Adrenaline skidded down her spine. "Sorenson. What brings you here?"

His smiled shifted, taking on a knowing slant. "Your friend here. And you. Dex sent me."

Somewhere behind them, a door opened and voices floated down the hall. Sorensen's hand slid inside his jacket as he looked past them.

Cabrini laid him out with a rapid jab-and-uppercut combination.

She froze for a heartbeat, then pushed open the service door. They dragged Sorenson onto the landing.

"Give me your cuffs." Cabrini held out his hand.

She stared at him as he crouched over Dex's assistant. *Dex sent me.* Three little words confirmed what she'd been denying since the cabin exploded. She still didn't want to believe it.

Dex *was* involved.

Reality mashed her heart to the pit of her stomach, and her exhale had a decided catch to it. With shaking hands, she dug into the Coach bag and pulled out a small bundle of plastic zip-tie restraints.

She avoided Cabrini's intent look. Thankfully, he didn't make any comment as he took a couple of ties.

She forced her fingers to stop trembling as she threaded a restraint around Sorenson's ankles and pulled it snug. After a few deep breaths, she trusted her voice enough to ask, "Now what?"

"Now we get out of here." Cabrini pulled her to her feet and they headed down the stairs at a fast clip. "By the way, who is he?"

"Dex's right-hand man."

"Did you recognize the other two?"

"No. I don't think—maybe."

He glanced at her as he swung around the railing, onto the next flight of stairs. "Nice definitive answer."

"Yeah, well, I haven't had any caffeine yet, so it's the best I can do."

Cabrini stopped at the next landing and pulled her into his arms. "Okay. Let's take a few seconds and assess the situation."

She wanted to fight against his embrace. "I don't need you to hold me up." Being held felt so good. Too good.

"No, but I want to, so indulge me."

"Suit yourself."

He chuckled, and his warm breath teased her neck. "We've got Dex's assistant trussed up in the stairwell four floors above us. There are two thugs in our room."

"Plus at least two others covering the hotel entrances."

"Right. We need to get by them and open the safe-deposit box."

We. She'd never worked as part of a "we." The ease with which they'd slipped into the process surprised her. They made a good team.

For how long? She stiffened her back. "There's still the question of what bank holds the box."

"True. A little research will take care of that." He loosened his hold on her and allowed her to step away. "Any suggestions how we get out of here?"

"We split up." She started down the stairs. "Two guys can't cover all the entrances. Odds are in our favor that one of us will get by one of them."

"Unless they have reinforcements."

"You're just a ray of sunshine, aren't you?"

"And you're limping."

"Yippee-skippee." She scowled over her shoulder at him. "A new dimension to my disguise."

"You think that'll be enough to throw them off?" He pushed in front of her and blocked the way. "Sit down. I want to check your ankle."

"It's nothing. I'll have it walked off by the time we get to the bottom."

"Sit." He pushed down on her shoulders.

She sat with her arms crossed and a scowl on her face. He ignored her peeve as he tested her ankle. "It seems to be okay. At least there's no swelling."

"You should try listening to me sometime."

"Okay, I'm listening. How do you suggest we proceed?"

"Oh, fine. Leave the hard stuff to me." She ran her hands through her hair. "First step is getting out of this building."

She waited for him to make a smart comeback. He didn't say anything, just rubbed her ankle with his warm hands.

The sensations generated by his touch mingled with an unexpected appreciation of his presence. Having a partner had some definite pluses. Even if it was only temporary.

Time enough for that reality later. Right now, escape took priority. "We've got three lobby levels with access to the public elevators. Those elevators open on both the street level and skyway level."

Cabrini glanced down the stairwell.

"I don't know where these stairs come out." She answered his unasked question. "And I don't like going down a blind path."

"Right. Let's stick with what we know. Five possible intercept points. If there's someone watching every level—"

"We're screwed." She stood. Sitting and talking wasn't getting them anywhere. They needed to move. "They'll be watching for a couple, so we can't go together."

"There has to be another way."

"There is. You noticed the escalators in the lobby, by the hotel guest elevators?" She waited for his nod.

"They end on the second floor, outside of the hotel, in a skyway hall of the City Center stores."

"So one of us goes that way, hoping to get by the lobby thug."

"While the other goes down the elevators and avoids the street thug."

Cabrini stopped. "Okay, suppose we both manage to get past them. Then what?"

"We find the bank."

He shook his head. "I need a phone. While we're getting out of here, the office can start the research. With a little luck, they'll have the answer by the time we're on the street."

She pulled out her phone and handed it to him.

He handed it back to her. "Does that mean what I think it means?"

The No Signal icon glowed in the display. "It figures." She shoved the phone back into her purse.

Somewhere above them, a door opened. A woman's scream bounced down the cement walls.

"Shiloh. Someone found Sorenson."

"Let's get out of here before they find us."

Two more flights and they were at the door to the fifth-floor lobby.

"I'll take the escalator." Cabrini stood in front of the door. "Meet me at the library. We can research banks there." He smoothed a hand over her hair and cupped the back of her head. "One more thing."

"What?"

"Be careful." He kissed her, one of his slow nibbling, never-quite-reaching-the-lips kisses.

She loved those kisses. "You, too."

They slipped through the door and headed in their assigned directions.

Frank spotted Lobby Thug almost immediately. He sat on one of the fourth-floor lobby couches, watching people come and go.

Acting like a casual tourist, Frank made a pretense of looking around the lobby as he moved from one escalator to the next. The whole time, Lobby Thug held his attention.

Better watch it. Dubbing their tails with silly tags didn't lessen the danger they presented.

As if proving the point, Lobby Thug rose from his seat and headed for the escalator.

Frank walked down the moving stairs. One of many weak points in this plan was how little used the escalator was. There would be no blending in with the crowd, because there was no crowd.

Footsteps sounded behind him. He threw a casual glance back as he rounded the corner onto the last flight. Lobby Thug had definitely followed him.

Smoked glass doors blocked the bottom of the steps. Frank pushed through them, and paused long enough to get his bearings.

To the left was a mostly empty hallway that doglegged into the shopping center. To the right, a skyway crossed the street.

He caught a flash of Elf's lavender jacket as she came from the hotel's outside elevator bank and started across the glass enclosed bridge.

A casually dressed man trailed after her.

Instinct said go right, follow her, be there if she ran into trouble and needed help.

Training said divide and conquer. Elf could handle herself. Better than most people. She'd be fine. He needed to get moving.

He turned left.

* * *

The nape of Angel's neck tingled, a dead giveaway someone followed her. She increased her pace a little, blending with other skyway pedestrians. Once she got into Marshall Field's she'd have plenty of exits to choose from and more opportunity for cover.

Foot traffic was light in the store. When she got to the men's casual clothing department, she left the main aisle and wandered among the racks and displays.

She picked a shirt off a table and used it as cover as she scoped out the area. A bank of mirrors reflected the image of a man wearing a lightweight jacket. The same man had been loitering near the hotel entrance.

"Isn't that a great color?" A salesman stopped beside her.

"It's very nice." Inspiration struck. She turned her back to her shadow. "Maybe you can help me with something."

"Of course. What are you looking for?"

"Nothing just now, but can you tell me if that man by the mirrors—" she kept her hand by her shoulder as she pointed behind her "—the one with the olive-green-ish jacket on. Is he a member of your store security? Because he's been following me, and it seems kind of creepy."

The salesman looked over her shoulder. "I've never seen him before. Let's go make a call."

Frank ducked into a tourist-trap store. The tall shelves and racks of Minnesota-themed shirts, mugs and trinkets provided a wealth of kitschy cover. As soon as his tail passed the entrance, Frank stepped back into the mall.

He wanted to maintain a safe distance, but he needed to keep the guy in sight.

Not as easy as it might seem. He'd already disappeared.

Frank stopped outside a jewelry store, pretending to look at the gaudy diamonds as he watched for Lobby Thug's reappearance.

A few seconds passed, and his wait bore fruit. LT stepped out of a store two doors down. And turned in his direction.

Frank stepped into the jewelry store.

Chapter 13

Angel watched from a discreet distance, expressing a suitable level of gratitude to the salesman for his assistance in capturing the "stalker." Store security hustled the suspect off to somewhere within the bowels of the building for a friendly chat. Now all she needed to do was get to the library and meet up with Cabrini.

Skyway traffic remained rather light, which would make it easy to spot anyone else trying to tail her. That same lack of pedestrians left her with a sense of vulnerability.

Street level would be better and quicker. She made her way out of the store, slipping on sunglasses against the bright summer sun.

Traffic definitely moved at a faster pace outside. Her new position had the added bonus of being able to check several skyways from a single location. Within a block, she spotted Frank crossing the street overhead.

A dark-suited man followed hot on his heels.

The building they entered provided several exit options. Since the public library was at the far end of Nicollet Mall, she laid odds Cabrini would head in that direction. She crossed the mall, dodging a city bus. As she pushed through the heavy doors of Gaviidae Common, she slipped off her jacket, turned it black side out and pulled it back on.

She didn't know yet exactly what she'd do, but she wouldn't desert Cabrini. *Please, please, please, let him come this way.*

Frank spotted Elf as he neared the atrium of the next building. She wore dark glasses and had somehow changed her jacket, but he recognized her as she climbed the escalator on the far side of the atrium.

A few days ago, he might not have seen through the changes. Now, all it took was a slight tilt of her head and he knew, without a doubt, it was her.

Another bunch of stores surrounded them, but LT probably wouldn't fall for that ruse a second time. He needed to shake him for good.

Elf reached the second floor and he spotted another addition to her disguise repertoire. As she headed in his general direction, her white cane tapped a gentle beat on the marble floor.

They passed without any acknowledgement. A moment later, he heard the thud of colliding bodies and the raised tones of an indignant British woman.

"You clumsy oaf!" the familiar voice railed.

Atta girl, Elf.

A muttered response.

"Typical American male, walking about with no regard for anyone else. I suppose you intend to just leave me here with everything strewn all about and no help putting things to rights."

Frank checked out the scene as he headed down the escalator. LT crouched on the floor, gathering the spilled contents of the briefcase, never looking above the white cane. Elf stood over him like an avenging angel as a security guard trotted over to investigate the commotion.

Out on the street, Frank considered waiting, then decided against it. One thing he knew for sure after four days—Elf could handle herself and just about anything thrown her way. She'd handled him with little difficulty.

Which proved to be a new and interesting experience. Unlike the safe women he normally dated, Elf challenged him. She came as close to an equal as he'd ever found. The possibilities for their relationship existed on an entirely different level.

And she wouldn't appreciate him waiting for her, as though she were anything less than completely capable.

They had agreed to rendezvous at the library. That's where he needed to go.

The new public library anchored on the north end of Nicollet Mall was a showplace of cutting-edge technology. Angel scanned the banks of computers that allowed patrons to search the library system's extensive holdings with a few simple keystrokes.

She spotted Cabrini logged in at one of the terminals. She sat at the next desk. "Nice view."

"Hadn't noticed."

"You didn't plan to sit where you can see everyone who enters the area?"

He shrugged. "Is that how you found me?"

"I found you because I figured the computers would be the most logical place for looking up information." She slid her chair closer to him. "Speaking of which, have you found anything yet?"

"Just getting started. It looks like your mother's bank merged with another one around the same time as your father's death."

"Murder."

Cabrini leaned back in his chair and studied her.

She balled one hand into a fist. Twenty years, and the pain still held a raw ache for her. *It must be a hundred times worse for Mom. I need to find who killed him. And why.*

Cabrini's warm hand covered hers. "Shortly after the merger, the bank moved locations."

The small comfort of his touch eased the tightness in her chest. "I've been trying to figure out how Mom could have kept this secret so long. Banks require regular contact from a customer or they consider an account or a box abandoned, don't they?"

He returned his attention to the computer. "Yes, they do."

"This is just a wild-goose chase." She pushed her sunglasses to the top of her head and rubbed her eyes. "There is no safe-deposit box. If there ever was one, the contents have long since disappeared."

"Maybe not."

"But she hasn't gone to the bank in years."

"Safe-deposit boxes are usually—almost always— tied to a bank account. Maybe you never noticed a charge on the statement."

"Yeah, right. That's real likely."

"I'm not ready to give up on this track just yet. Are you?"

She sighed. Her shoulders sagged and she scratched her fingers through her hair. "I hate wasting time. We should go to Dex's office and have it out with him. Find out what's really going on and be done with it."

"Nice fantasy. Don't think he's real anxious to see us. At least, not on our schedule."

"Maybe...." She straightened in her chair. "Saskatoon."

Cabrini looked up. "What?"

"I must be brain-dead." Excitement danced along her arms.

"You just remembered something, didn't you?"

"Yepper. A savings account that shrinks a little each year because of an annual service charge."

"Why do you keep it?"

"Because every year when I mutter something about closing it and putting the money someplace where it'd do some good, my mother stops me. 'It was your father's. Leave it be,' she says."

"And you've left the money sitting there."

"It wasn't such a huge amount that it would make a big difference. There didn't seem to be any harm in letting her have that final connection, especially if it gave her some peace of mind."

"Where is it?"

"Back down Nicollet a few blocks."

"What are we waiting for?"

"For you to log off the computer and empty the cache."

He nodded. "No sense in leaving behind clues."

The safe-deposit box area of Aegis National Bank sat off to the side of the large, marble lobby, behind a heavy glass door. Two gray leather chairs sat against one narrow wall, and a chest-high marble service counter guarded the vault entrance.

The woman assigned to the area greeted them with a pleasant and impersonal smile when they entered. "May I help you?"

"Yes." Angel stepped to the counter. "I have something of a dilemma and I'm hoping you might be able to help."

Her words triggered a subtle chill in the banker's attitude.

She took a deep breath. Just act natural and calm, same as for any facade. The worst the keeper of the vault could do would be to say no. "You see, my mother gave me this key." She held it out to the woman.

"Yes?" Tillie the Hun wasn't going to volunteer any help.

"Well, you see, she's had the box since before this building was built. In fact, it was originally in one of the smaller banks this bank acquired nearly twenty years ago."

"There's nothing I can do about that."

"Well, no, of course there isn't. But perhaps you could tell me if this key fits one of the boxes here."

"No."

"No, you can't tell me, or no, it doesn't match?"

"Are you an authorized signer on the account?"

Progress. Sort of. "Yes."

Tillie slapped a card on the counter. "Sign this."

She signed and slid the card back across the counter. Tillie went to a bank of card files and flipped through the contents.

Angel turned and caught Cabrini ogling her legs. It was all she could do to not tug on her skirt. The length had seemed perfectly suitable, modest even, when she'd dressed that morning. Now the skirt seemed shorter by the minute, as his gaze wandered from her ankles to her hips and back.

She shifted her weight from one foot to the other, blaming her discomfort on the pumps she wore.

"How's your ankle?"

"Fine." Memories of the previous night's foot rub that had begun so innocently warmed her cheeks and neck.

"It doesn't match." Tillie's return put an end to any more reminiscing.

"I'm sorry?"

"Your signature does not match the signature on record."

"Could I see the record?"

"Certainly not."

They had not come this far to quit. Angel took a slow breath. "It's just that I think I was about twelve years old when I signed the card. My signature has changed some since then."

"Minors are not allowed to enter into contracts." Tillie latched onto that bit of information. "If you were under eighteen years of age when you signed a card contracting ownership of a safe-deposit box, it was an act of fraud."

Okay, not exactly the obstacle I expected. "There were extenuating circumstances."

"Of course there were." The response left no room for doubt of her opinion.

"Well, there must be a way to sort this out." Angel stood straighter, bringing every inch of her height into play. "Surely there are other ways to verify identity."

"The signature does not match. There's nothing I can do." Tillie headed back to her desk.

"Wait a second."

"Was there something else you wanted?"

"Yes, I want to see the contents of the box."

"You must be an authorized signer on the account to access the box."

"I am."

"Your signature does not match."

Well, that had been a quick round-trip. "Had a lot of training on handwriting analysis, have you?"

Cabrini turned her away from the counter with a firm hand on her shoulder. "Relax."

"But we need to get into that box." Denied access made it seem more urgent than she'd realized.

"We will."

His calm response didn't alleviate her tension. "We need to get into that box before someone else finds a way to bre—"

He cut her off with a kiss.

"What was that for?" she asked when he released her.

His low tone didn't carry beyond her. "To stop you before you said something that landed security on our butts like the proverbial ton."

"There are other ways to get me to stop talking."

"True, but they aren't nearly as much fun." He gave her another quick kiss.

"Fine." She shook her head at his boyish grin. "You got me to stop, now what do you suggest?"

"When the front line doesn't give you the answer you want, you go to the next level."

Of course. Like that would be easy. Nothing had been easy since taking Cabrini into custody. She took a deep breath and turned back to the counter.

"I'd like to speak to the manager." She put as much reason and calm into her request as she could muster.

As if on cue, the glass door opened. Only, rather than a business-suited banker, a uniformed security guard entered.

Tillie rose from her desk.

"What the…?" Angel gaped at the banker.

The woman stood with shoulders back, head raised to an imperious angle and a steel rod down her spine. "Either this woman is trying to illegally gain access to a box or she illegally rented the box."

The guard turned an impassive eye on her. Cabrini slipped his arm around her waist.

Several hours, three management levels and untold

repetitions of the situation later, the bank manager finally accompanied them back to the vault area.

Tillie was slightly less of a Hun. Once the manager had thoroughly assured her, and overseen the completion of a new signature card, she escorted Angel back to the secured area.

Butterflies performed acrobatic loop-the-loops in her stomach when the box slid out of the slot. The sensation caught her off guard.

Tillie led her to a small room. "Take as much time as you need." Her attitude had certainly been adjusted.

The door of the privacy room clicked shut, and Angel rested her hands on the flat, metal box. How long had it been since anyone looked in it? Who had been that last person? Her father?

Her hands shook. The emotions seeped into her awareness one by one. Sadness as she relived the loss of her father. Anger at the arsonist responsible for his death. Fear that the contents of the box would be worthless. Until she opened the box, for all she knew, it could be empty.

Where was Cabrini and his assurances when she really needed him?

Needed him. She could admit that, there in the tiny room, where there were no witnesses. Four days with the man and she wanted him with her, felt something missing when he was gone.

They thought so much alike, it sometimes seemed as though they were connected at the brain.

If she didn't watch out, she'd start to rely on him. And then he'd leave.

She hadn't wanted to get involved with a man for exactly that reason. She didn't want to lose her independence, get used to the strength of having a partner, only to lose that person. Her mother was a living example of the kind of hell that could create.

Her life might not be perfect, but at least it was of her own making, not the result of an ill-fated love.

She didn't need Cabrini to be complete. She had her job, she had her mother. Maybe someday she'd have a cat.

The hard, metal edges of the safe deposit box dug into her clenched hands. She needed to concentrate on the task at hand.

A fine tremor ran through her fingers. She took a deep, cleansing breath. There was nothing to be concerned about. Whatever the box held, it wouldn't change the world.

The lid opened on silent hinges. She laid the contents out on the desk then sat back in the hard chair, staring at what her mother had been so desperate for her to see.

Patrick Donovan's legacy consisted of an envelope with black-and-white negatives and a flat box containing a reel of audiotape.

She slipped the contents into her briefcase, closed the box and opened the door.

Tillie returned the box to its slot in the vault wall, then ushered Angela back to the lobby.

Her high heels beat out a quick tempo on the marble floor. Cabrini stood, and a sense of relief warmed her. Opening the box had been harder than she'd imagined it could be. It would be good to have a partner to help figure out what the contents meant.

"Something's been bothering me, Elf." Frank held open the door to the street as they exited the bank.

"Just one thing?"

"Well, no, actually. There are several things, but I thought I'd start with one."

"Okay, what's the one thing?"

"Did you tell your mother or her companion where we were staying?"

She slipped her sunglasses into place. "No. I figure the less they know about the particulars of whatever I'm working on, the better off we all are."

"Who did you meet with while I checked in at the hotel?"

"No one. I worked out at the club, then went to the salon to get my hair colored." She frowned. "What are you getting at?"

"How did Sorenson and the thug brigade find us?"

The streetlight changed and they stopped at the crosswalk. Elf turned to him. "You think I leaked our location to someone who sent them?"

"No. You're too good at your job to make that kind of slip."

"Gee, thanks."

"Which leaves us with, how did they figure out where we were?"

The light turned green and they moved with the pedestrian traffic.

"Do you think someone's been following us?"

"If they are, I haven't spotted them."

"Considering I followed you for a week…" She let the comment trail off.

"I was careless, I admit it. But I wasn't expecting my cover to be blown. Now I know it has been and I've been watching very closely. No one followed us until the thug brothers showed up."

"Okay, then we've got a couple things to figure out this afternoon. You can work on how we were found, and I'll work on the contents of the box."

"Speaking of which…"

"We need to get to a sound studio."

"I assume you'll tell me why, eventually." He motioned her ahead of him through the hotel's revolving door. He scanned the entrance and the skyway-level balcony. There didn't appear to be anyone other than the valet and bellmen hanging around.

The bell captain responded to his signal. "Yes, sir?"

"Could you bring our car around, please?" Frank handed him a ticket.

"Certainly."

They drifted to a corner of the entrance that sheltered them from prying eyes and still afforded access to a quick getaway. He slipped his arm around Elf's waist and pulled her close.

A dull clang announced the arrival of an elevator. Tension hummed through his nerves, all of his senses on alert, as he watched half a dozen people get off the elevator. They wore convention badges and were engaged in an animated debate. None of them belonged to the thug brigade.

Elf sighed. She'd been wound as tight as he was. Nothing about the day had gone according to plan. He would have liked a little more one-on-one time with her, alone in their room, but that wasn't likely to happen anytime soon.

He settled for holding her close, breathing in her scent as they waited.

The car arrived. This time Elf took the wheel. "My brain hurts. I need some caffeine."

He glanced at his watch. Mid-afternoon, and neither of them had eaten. "Food wouldn't hurt, either. Maybe we can find a phone book and locate a sound studio while we eat."

"No need. I've got it covered."

He watched her navigate the traffic streaming towards the Uptown neighborhood. She'd been quiet ever since leaving the bank. Something ate at her. He could probably come pretty close to figuring out what, but he'd rather she told him.

"Any idea what's on the tape?"

"It could be an old recording of songs. Maybe voice letters from when Dad was away in the service. It may all mean nothing."

Or it could be the key to everything. Elf kept wanting to fight the reality he knew they faced. They didn't have much time, but he'd give her what he could to come to terms with Dexter's betrayal.

"Care to share what else you found in the deposit box?"

Several blocks passed before she answered. "Some negatives."

There was more. He could hear it in her voice but until she said the words… "Talk to me, Elf. What's eating at you?"

"Everything. How did they find us? Who sent them? Why?"

"We know who and I have a pretty solid idea why, but you don't want to listen to that theory."

"It doesn't seem possible. There has to be something more to it. Sorenson could be behind this. Maybe he's setting up Dex."

"That could be possible, I suppose." Possible, but not likely. "What about the negatives? Any idea what's on them?"

"I couldn't tell. The images were too small and the light in the bank wasn't exactly ideal."

"Add photo lab to our list of needs."

"No. I've—"

"Got it covered," he finished for her.

The slightest of grins tugged at her mouth as she pulled into the parking ramp attached to Calhoun Square. "We can eat someplace here."

There was a variety of restaurants to choose from, and Frank led the way to the wrap sandwich shop. "This will be faster."

They ordered and settled at a table off to the side, where they could see the mall and street entrances to the shop.

Elf picked at her sandwich. "I've got a friend who's something of a techno-nerd. She might be able to help us with the film and the tape."

"Do you trust her?"

"She's helped me a number of times. In fact, you met her at the CC Club."

"The uptown babe is your techno-nerd?"

"Appearances can be deceiving."

"That's become painfully clear to me on this assignment." He wadded his food wrappers into a tight bundle. "So what is she going to do for us?"

"Two things, I hope. Use her computer setup to scan the negatives and give us prints. While she's doing that for us, I'll use her audio equipment to listen to the tape."

"Your friend has a reel-to-reel machine just lying around?"

"That's her main business, actually. Her sound studio is quite popular with a lot of the ad agencies and production companies in town."

"A buddy who does car disguises, a friend with computer and sound specialties… Any chance you have an electronics expert in your address book?"

"Sure, along with race car driver, martial arts master, weaver, photographer. I'll be calling him if Tina can't work her magic on the film."

"You've got quite a collection of talented friends."

She shrugged. "We help each other out when we can. It's a good—Heidelberg."

"What?" He glanced around the room without being obvious.

"Thug brothers are back. How did they find us?"

"Let's worry about that later. Right now, we need to lose them. Again."

"That's not going to be so easy."

"We did it before." He stood and led the way out to the street.

"Yeah, but this time my thug has something in his hand, and he's watching it pretty close."

"I noticed. It might be a tracking device of some kind."

"You think we're bugged?"

"How else could they find us? The real question is, how did they bug us? And which one of us?"

Chapter 14

"They must have planted something when we were at the hotel." Angel watched over her shoulder as they turned the corner. Her stomach flip-flopped. She slowed to a stop. "Which means it's in the car. We've got to find another means of transportation."

"I'll buy the bug theory, but I think you're off on the location."

"If not the car, where do you think they planted it?" She backtracked to an entrance they'd passed. "Let's see if we can lose them in the bookstore."

Cabrini followed her in and they wove their way through the tall book stacks. "How did they find us at the hotel so easy? No one followed us there. If the tracer is on the car, there's no way they could have pinpointed where we were after we parked."

Angel scrubbed her hands through her hair. Everything he said made sense. She hated that, hated the implications. "Okay. If it's something that allowed them to follow us to the hotel, then it has to be something we carried with us."

He held out his hand and flicked his fingers. "Let me see the car keys for a second."

"You think…" She dug in her purse and pulled out the key ring. "In this?"

"It makes sense. What else are you likely to carry with you after you've parked?" He studied the key fob for a moment then pried it open. "Bingo."

Nestled inside the casing was a tiny transmitter. Cabrini pulled it out and snapped the fob back together. "Who would have access to these keys?"

A cold fist clenched around Angel's stomach. "It's a short list. Mom doesn't drive."

"That leaves you and your mother's companion. Has anyone else driven it?"

"Mechanics at the dealership, maybe, when we take it in for service."

"What dealer did you pick up the car from?"

"I didn't. Dex had it delivered. But that was almost two years ago."

"He could have planted it then."

No, that was too far-fetched. She started to tell him that when he motioned for silence. He whispered, "They just came in."

Cabrini led their way through several rows of books, pausing every few feet to check the progress of their trackers. They made it to the video section and stopped again. Laying the tracer on a row of DVDs, he leaned close. "I love irony, don't you?"

She looked at the movie title. *Enemy of the State.* Will Smith, Gene Hackman, bugs and tracers, covert operations—one of her all-time favorite movies. A smile caught her by surprise. She turned to say something, and discovered Cabrini still leaned close. His lips brushed hers. A tiny shiver danced down her back.

"Let's get out of here." He laced his fingers through hers and led her out of the store, up an escalator to the second floor and out to the parking ramp.

"Don't you want to wait and see if you're right?"

"No need." He opened the passenger door for her. "I know I am."

"About the tracer, maybe." The door closing interrupted her. When Cabrini settled behind the wheel, she continued. "You don't know for sure who planted it."

"Sorenson as good as told us." He brushed the back of his fingers over her hand as he reversed out of their parking spot. "Sooner or later, you're going to have to accept that maybe Dex isn't the great guy you want him to be."

"I know." She leaned her head against the leather seat back. "It's just that...I don't understand why. Why, after all these years of helping out, watching over us, treating us like his own family, why would he turn on me?"

"Maybe we can figure that out when we hear what's on the tape." He stopped the car at the parking ramp exit. "Where are we going?"

"Tina's studio. Take a right and head towards the lake."

She directed him on a circuitous route around two of the city's lakes. Other than her directions, they drove in silence. Cabrini left her to her thoughts. She avoided thinking.

After parking on a residential street not far from Lake of the Isles, she led him down a block and around a corner. Many of the houses they walked by in the next couple of blocks were older, dating from the early 1900s, with stained-glass windows and wraparound porches. They were homes built to escape the city and raise a large family. Now they housed upwardly mobile, double-income couples.

Cabrini followed her around another corner to a tall, weathered wood gate. The slightly askew sign proclaimed Tina's Tunes. Through the gate, a path led around a small flower garden to the carriage house that had been converted into a state-of-the-art sound studio.

A snippet of the song "Welcome to my World" announced their arrival when she pushed the door open.

"Yo, Tina," she called with a Brooklyn accent.

The soft murmur of voices floated down from the studio loft. Footsteps followed. "Hey, kiddo. What's up?"

Angel met her partway up the stairs. "Sorry to bother you, but is there any chance I can tap your audio expertise?"

"Sure. I'm booked for another hour with this client, then I'm free."

"Could I borrow your computer and scanner in the meantime?"

"No problem." Tina frowned. "Are you okay?"

"Yeah. It's just been…" She shook her head. "I'll fill you in later."

Tina shrugged and headed back to her client. "You know where everything is."

It was challenging, but Frank did his best to stay out of the way as Elf moved around the closet-sized office, turning on equipment, booting up the computer system and opening programs.

Each time she brushed against him, he wanted to pull her into his arms and hold her. His reaction bordered on insanity.

The last thing she'd tolerate would be him trying to coddle her.

Not that that changed his wanting.

She finally settled into the desk chair. He leaned against the credenza behind her.

With easy familiarity, she arranged a strip of negatives on the scanner. In a matter of minutes, she filled the screen with several images.

He leaned closer to get a better look, and her scent wound through his awareness.

She shifted in the chair and, for a fraction of a second, he thought she moved closer to him. Then she reached for another strip of negatives and put them on the scanner. He sighed, feeling just a bit foolish at enjoying the moment while she seemed to be oblivious to his reactions.

The process continued until she had all the film scanned. Then she sifted through the images, selecting, enlarging and studying each frame. Some she copied and set aside. Others she burned to a CD and closed.

When she finished, three pictures remained on the screen. She selected one and blew it up until it filled the large monitor.

Three men sat around a table, drinks in front of them, a cigar leaking a plume of smoke into the already hazy air. They appeared to be in a bar, but the photographer had zoomed in close. Little of the background remained to help identify a specific location.

"Do you recognize any of them?" He broke the silence.

She leaned back in the chair and ran both hands through her hair, leaving spikes standing on end and looking a little more like the Elf he knew and loved.

"This one." She pointed at one man. "That's Dex. The man beside him," she continued, her finger caressing the screen. "He's my father."

Frank rested one hand on her shoulder and gave a little squeeze. Small comfort against the loss so evident in her voice.

She took a deep breath. "The other man...I'm not sure. It seems like I should."

"The film has to be nearly twenty years old. There's no reason you'd recognize a buddy of your dad's from back then. You might not have even met him."

"But he looks vaguely familiar." She framed the third man's face and enlarged it several times. The image degraded, but that worked to their advantage. The softer edge to the man's features aged him.

Elf squinted as she studied the picture. "Sanders?" A frown wrinkled her forehead.

"Who?" The name sounded familiar.

"I think...Dr. Sanders." She leaned away from the screen. "He took care of Mom, practically since the day of Dad's murder. I don't know how we would have made it through those early days without him and Dex there to help."

Frank remembered then. The name had been included in the case notes assembled by The Diamond Group. The doctor had been responsible for the initial misdiagnosis and improper medication of Maryam Donovan. The circumstances surrounding the doctor's sudden disappearance took on extra importance with this new information.

He backed away from revealing another betrayal. Not yet. He wouldn't do that to her. Instead, he redirected her focus for the moment. "What I'm curious about is who took the picture, and why?"

Elf looked at him. He refused to meet the question in her eyes. She turned back to the computer and expanded one of the other shots. "This is essentially the same shot, just a wider angle."

They both leaned closer to the screen, studying the details, trying to make out some clue.

"Is that a mirror on the wall?" He pointed at a section of the background.

She marked the section and blew it up. "Yeah. The image is pretty grainy, but we are seeing the reverse of the foreground. That's Dad."

"Do you think we can make out who else was there?"

"Maybe." She looked from the computer screen to him. "You're thinking we might be able to pinpoint the photographer?"

"It's a long shot, I know, but worth trying."

She shrugged and repeated the enlarging process. "Then what? I get that Dad must have known the photographer to wind up with the film. But there's no guarantee I'll be able to ID him."

"No, but maybe your mother will."

Her hands stopped moving over the keyboard.

"What?" he asked when she didn't say anything.

"I'm not sure showing Mom these pictures would be wise. She's—"

"Fragile, I know." He turned the desk chair, forcing Angel to face him. "Your mother may not be as delicate as you think. You said yourself that she seems stronger, more normal."

"Even so, I don't want to hurt her. If these pictures bring back bad memories for her…"

He brushed one hand over her hair, smoothing down the spikes. "We don't have to decide right now. Let's see what we have and then we can figure out where we go from there."

She turned back to the computer screen. "The image is degrading too much. Tina's way better at this. She might be able to do some techno-wizardry, or run a program of some sort and pull something out of it."

Footsteps overhead and down the stairs signaled the

end of the sound session in Tina's studio. "Welcome to my World" accompanied the departure of the client.

The office door opened.

Frank stood and turned to face Tina. Her eyes rounded in surprise. "You?" She stepped away, out of reach.

He smiled. "None other."

Elf pushed him out of her way. "I'm sorry I didn't say anything when we got here, but I didn't want to get into long explanations. Especially not when you had clients waiting."

"Well, they're gone now, and you can take all the time you want. I'm dying to hear."

"Maybe later, after a pitcher of margaritas." A blush warmed Elf's cheeks.

Frank held back a chuckle, knowing she'd probably reward him with an elbow to the diaphragm again. She had sharp elbows, and he'd just as soon forgo the experience.

"You're on, chiquita." Tina nodded towards the computer. "What have you got for me?"

"A couple things." Relief eased the tension lines from Elf's face. She slid back onto the office chair. "I've scanned in a couple negs I'm hoping you can do a little image refining on. But first," she said, as she reached into her briefcase on the credenza and pulled out a flat box about twelve inches square. "I need to hear what's on this tape."

"No problem. C'mon upstairs." Tina led the way back up the carpeted stairs.

A soundproof booth filled one end of the studio. Facing the booth, a huge sound console dominated the room. Shelves filled with compact discs lined one entire side wall. The opposite side displayed framed album covers, awards and movie memorabilia.

Elf and Tina settled into chairs in front of the console. The only place left to sit was an ugly, olive drab, overstuffed easy chair. As soon as he sat, the biggest, fluffiest gray cat he'd ever seen leaped into his lap, swished its tail in his face and settled down to watch.

"I hope you're not allergic." Tina glanced up from threading the audiotape onto the reel-to-reel tape deck. She exchanged a raised eyebrow look with Elf. "So, he's okay."

"Yeah." Elf swiveled to look at him. "I guess he is."

"What?"

"Czar has very discerning taste," Elf explained. "He doesn't like most people. You just passed the ultimate test."

"The cat sat in my lap."

"Yepper. Most people, he ignores. If he takes a dislike, he's been known to attack."

"Those people," Tina joined in, "I don't book with again."

"You only work with people your cat approves of?"

She nodded as she slipped on a set of headphones.

He looked back at Elf. "You just now decided I was okay?"

"You have to admit, we got off to a less than auspicious start. An impartial read—"

"From a cat—"

"—is good confirmation."

Thank you, Czar. He scratched under the cat's chin and triggered a loud purr.

Tina pushed, turned and twiddled the controls in front of her. Finally, she pulled off the headphones. "We're ready."

Elf tensed and leaned forward.

"I'm going to let it run, and dump it to digital as it goes," Tina explained. "Then we'll have a copy to work with right from the start."

She handed a notepad and pen to Elf. "Why don't you log it, so we can pinpoint any sections of particular interest."

The reels on the tape deck turned. No one said anything as voices came over the speakers.

Angel checked the time code clock as the voice from her childhood memory filled the room.

You have the proof we need? Her father, his tone harsher, colder than he'd ever used around her, but still recognized in a heartbeat.

Here are the prints from your meeting. Another man's voice. Paper rustled and a few seconds of silence followed. *Do you have a safe place to keep the negatives?*

She tried to make notes as Tina monitored the sound levels, but her hand refused to move as words washed over her. When Cabrini took the pen and pad from her, she didn't protest. Her hands balled into fists, and every muscle across her back tightened.

The taped voices detailed a series of meetings between Marvin Dexter and various businessmen and property owners. Shortly after each meeting, the individual fell victim to an arsonist's torch.

One to two months after each fire, Dex seemed to tap into sweetheart deals, such as twenty acres of northern lakeshore property at a fraction of the normal cost.

The last meeting documented on the tape involved a clinic owned by Dr. Sanders.

The end of the tape ran through the tape deck.

Silence. Except for the denials her heart screamed.

She could feel Tina and Cabrini watching her. She shook out her cramped hands.

"Whoa." Tina's soft exhalation sounded loud in the room. "Was that…?"

"My father." The voice of a ghost. She stood.

"Elf?" Cabrini's voice sounded so far away, but she could feel his touch as he brushed her hair away from her eyes. His thumb wiped across her cheek, smearing moisture in its wake.

Tears? When had she started crying?

He pulled her into his arms and she accepted the warmth and strength he provided. She wanted to stay there. She didn't want to listen to the tape again, hear the voices again. Know the depth of Marvin Dexter's betrayal.

"Did you get everything transferred to a digital file?" Cabrini's voice vibrated in his chest beneath her ear.

If Tina answered, she didn't hear.

"I need photocopies of the log and a copy of that audio file to overnight to my office tonight."

"Office?" This time, Tina's response broke through the buzzing in her ears.

The tape proved Cabrini had been right. Dex would stop at nothing to reach his goal. Twenty years ago, he'd killed his partner to cover up a string of arsons that had become a lucrative side career.

History nearly repeated itself when the lakeside cabin funded by those arsons had gone up in flames.

She released an unsteady breath and stepped away from Cabrini. He kept hold of her hand, not letting her completely separate herself from him.

"Angel?" Tina watched them from her chair by the console.

She nodded. "It's okay. He's a private investigator. Mom hired him."

"Your mother?"

She waved off Tina's question. "I'll explain later." Adrenaline pumped through her veins with each new realization of what they had in their possession. "Right now, you need to burn two copies of that audio file onto CD, then wipe every trace of the file from your equipment."

She pulled away from Cabrini's loose hold. "We can't leave any evidence that we've been here."

He nodded. "I'll take care of the computer downstairs."

"Tina—" she turned to her friend "—you can't tell anyone about the tape. Or the pictures. You never saw them, you never heard anything, we haven't talked in over a week."

"It's that serious, isn't it?"

"Worse. I never should have come here. I'm sorry."

"Hey, I never saw you." She turned to her machines without another word.

Frank copied everything from the downstairs computer onto CDs.

He agreed with Elf one hundred percent. Any trace that they'd been at the sound studio could put Tina in danger.

They needed to clean up and get out of there.

The agency's tech gurus could take care of analyzing the file copies they sent. Not that he needed a report to know what they had. Hearing the tape, watching Elf's reactions, had been proof enough for him.

For her, too. Her tears had surprised him.

The speed of her recovery worried him.

Angel gave the studio one last idiot check sweep to make sure she had everything.

"Will you be okay?"

Tina's question brought her up short. Would she be okay? Maybe. Once she caught her father's murderer. She nodded and picked up the notepad used to log the tape.

That's all it took to trigger a flood of memories. Memories of what they'd heard. Memories of her childhood and the man her father had been.

Anger burned through her veins with each one.

Dexter would pay for what he'd done. For killing her father. For destroying her mother's life. For robbing Angel of two loving parents.

She forced her breathing to stay slow and even. She had to look calm, seem normal. Maintain the facade.

Tina, worry shadowing her eyes, laid the CDs and boxed tape reel on top of the notepad.

She slid the pile into her briefcase. "Double check your computers—make sure everything's gone."

"I will. Be careful."

"Of course." She gave her friend a quick hug.

Her next hurdle waited at the bottom of the stairs.

The way Cabrini stood guard over her only exit, she could tell he suspected something.

Smart man. But she was just as smart. She'd play the part he wanted to see, mislead with subterfuge, pretend they'd work the situation through as a team.

Then, the first opportunity she could make, she'd take care of her business her way.

Chapter 15

Frank saw through the expression on Elf's face. Did she really think she could fool him with the calm front?

If she did, she'd soon find out differently.

They left Tina's studio. Neither said a word as they retraced their winding path to where they'd parked the Lexus.

Birdsong and the rush and whoosh of evening traffic filled the silence. A gentle breeze laced the fragrance of roses and fresh mown grass with Elf's warm vanilla scent.

Elf and vanilla. The two were forever associated in his brain. Memories of their "introduction" held the odd juxtaposition of cold metal handcuffs with the gentle aroma of home baking.

Elf slowed her pace. "Looks like company."

Parking so far away from Tina's studio had seemed overly cautious at the time. Now he was glad they'd taken the extra step. A dark sedan, with two suspicious-looking occupants easily visible, sat parked between them and their car.

"I see them." It was possible there was no reason for suspicion. Then again, considering the run of luck they'd had so far today, the odds weren't in their favor. "I think it's time for that alternate mode of transportation."

She nodded and turned the next corner, heading for busy Hennepin Avenue. A bus pulled to a stop as they reached the intersection. "I hope you have change."

He followed her onto the bus, paid their fares and joined her on the back seat. "Any idea where this takes us?"

"Uptown. We can get off at the transit station."

"That's close to my place."

She nodded.

"Maybe we could stop in there?"

She shrugged.

"You aren't curious why? No issues with who we might run into? No concerns the place is being watched?"

She looked at him with a "What do you think?" expression.

"Look, we need to figure out our next step. You know we can't do that wandering around on the public transit system. A change of appearance wouldn't be a bad idea, either."

"And you think your room is a good place to do that?"

"At least we'd have a little privacy."

"I have another idea." She slipped her sunglasses in place. "I think it's time to split up."

"No." No way in hell was he going to let her go off by herself again. Not before they talked through a few things.

"It makes perfect sense. It worked back at the hotel. Apart, we have a better chance of eluding them."

"Apart, we're vulnerable. We need to stick together this time to watch each other's back."

That hit a nerve. Her shoulders stiffened and she lowered her chin. Looking over the top of her sunglasses, she narrowed her eyes. "Cabrini, I may be just a woman, but I have been working alone a very long time. One thing I do know is I do not need a man to do my work for me."

"I thought we'd gotten past that." When she didn't respond, he continued. "No, you don't need a man to help do your job. And I don't need a woman to help me with mine. Leave gender out of it and consider this— together, we're stronger. We have different resources to call on and complementary skills. Let's use that to our advantage."

"What do you have in mind?" she asked after a short silence.

"Regroup, reassess, respond."

"Meaning?"

"Meaning, we need to understand what we're dealing with and come up with a plan before we charge off anywhere."

The bus pulled into the transit station. Frank stood and held his hand out. She ignored it, brushed past him and left the bus.

Somehow, he needed to get through to her. She hadn't said a word about the tape and what they'd heard. Nothing to give him an idea of what she really felt beneath the calm face she insisted on presenting to the world. To him.

That's what ate at him most, the fact that she tried to hide her feelings from him.

When would she accept that it wouldn't work? Not

anymore. He knew hearing proof of Dexter's betrayal had to be eating at her. And he knew if she didn't let out the emotions, they would destroy her.

He cared too much about her to let that happen. Loved her too much.

They walked side by side to the large house where he'd rented a room. He slipped his hand under her elbow when her steps slowed. Her muscles flexed beneath his touch. He almost hoped she would resist. At least it would be a reaction of some sort.

She allowed him to escort her to the door of his second-floor room. He reached into his pocket. "Damn."

"What?"

"A little matter of the key." He'd long since lost track of it. The last time he could remember seeing it was at the cabin. "Don't suppose you have a lock pick in your bag?"

"What kind of professional do you think I am?" She dug into her briefcase, then offered him a slim leather case she'd pulled from the interior pocket.

He shook his head and stepped back to watch her handiwork. In a matter of seconds, she dealt with the lock and pushed the door open. He motioned her inside and followed.

She stopped just inside the door. Not that she had very many options of where to go. The room contained a bed, a chest of drawers and a bedside stand. Nothing adorned the drab, industrial beige of the walls. No personal items lay out to hint at what kind of person lived in the room.

"Be it ever so humble." He closed the door.

The click of the dead bolt lock startled Elf. As he watched her reaction, the room seemed to shrink, and the bed dominated the space. Awareness surged and it took a few seconds for him to get back in control of his body's response. *Later.* More important things needed to take precedence right now.

Things like coming up with new disguises yet again. And getting Elf to talk about the emotions she'd been hiding since they'd left the sound studio.

He tossed his blazer on top of the dresser and walked to the far side of the bed. "You might as well make yourself comfortable. We're going to be here for a while."

"How long a while?" She didn't move from her place by the door.

"As long as it takes to reinvent ourselves." He dropped to a crouch beside the bed and reached between the mattress and box spring.

His first day in the city, after moving into the rooming house, he'd stashed a few things he wouldn't need unless an emergency arose.

The whole day had been an emergency.

He pulled out the small bundle and unwrapped it.

Elf stepped closer. "You have a license for that?"

"Of course." He laid his Beretta pistol on the bed.

"What other goodies do you have?"

He went to the dresser, slid open the second from the bottom drawer and removed it. The envelope he'd taped there came loose with a single pull. His agency ID, Massachusetts driver's license and emergency cash joined the gun on the bed.

Elf sat on the edge of the mattress and picked up the ID. "I thought you didn't have any way to prove you worked for The Diamond Group."

"Not on me, I didn't. And, at the time, all I knew about you was that you served a mean knockout cocktail." He dropped a pair of handcuffs on top of the pile.

A blush crept up her neck and flowed over her cheeks.

The bed sagged when he sat beside her. He slipped

his hand over hers and held her in place when she tried
to edge away. "We need to come up with that plan. But
mostly, you need to talk."

"About what?"

"Don't play dumb, 'cause I'm not buying. You just
got hit with one hell of a shock."

"You're imagining things."

"I don't think so."

"Fine, then. Why don't you tell me what you think
it is that I must be feeling so we can deal with it? Then
maybe we can get down to the real issues."

She refused to look him in the eye. The muscle flexing along her jaw and the tension of her muscles under
his touch broadcast her emotions loud and clear.

After all they'd been through, she still wouldn't trust
him, still wouldn't share her emotions.

All right, then. He'd force her to see the evidence.
"Okay." He took a deep breath. "We have an audiotape
that starts out with the voice of a man who IDs himself
as Patrick Donovan. It's been nearly twenty years since
you've heard your father's voice."

"Ghosts don't frighten me."

"Quit trying to misdirect. We're not talking about
fear. Do you think that really was your father's
voice?"

She closed her eyes and tilted her head. He could
imagine she was replaying in her mind the voice they'd
heard on tape. After a few seconds, she nodded.

"Right. Then what we seem to have is the audio
record of a case he worked on with someone other than
his usual partner."

He paused, waiting for her to make a comment. She
pulled away from him and stood.

"He couldn't work with his partner because that's
who he was investigating."

She paced around the bed, staying just out of his reach.

"The tape and the photos build a pretty strong case against Marvin Dexter."

Her steps rang loud in the room. She kicked off the high-heeled pumps and continued walking, picking up speed with each pass.

"It doesn't take too much of a leap to conclude that Dexter must have realized he'd been found out. He took steps to prevent the outcome your father planned."

Elf ran her hands through her hair. He wanted to go to her, to pull her into his arms and comfort her. The bedspread bunched in his fists as he fought his impulses. Instead of holding her, he kept pummeling her with the evidence.

"You heard the tape. It ended with the documentation of your father's intention to confront the suspect."

"How could he do that?"

"What, Elf?"

"How could he go into that building, knowing what he knew?"

"I think he also knew it was up to him to put an end to the arson."

"It's not like he was the only person who knew."

"No, but he was the only person in a position to do anything. It was his duty."

"Duty." Elf spit the word. "A whole lot of good that duty did for him. For my mother. It cost her everything."

She was on the edge, so close to facing the truth. He waited for the dam to burst, ready to catch her, if she would allow it.

"How dare he do that to her?" Light shimmered off the tears in her eyes. "She loved him. She still loves him. When he didn't come home from his shift, when they told her he'd been killed, she lost the one thing that brought joy to her."

"The one thing?"

"Her life stopped when he died. She went through the motions, got through the funeral, all the legal processes, she did what she had to do." Her voice fell to a whisper. "Then it was done. Everyone left and it was just her."

"What about you?" His throat ached at the pain in her voice.

"I grew up."

"What did *you* lose, Angela?"

She turned to him. Pain, anger and understanding chased across her face, draining her cheeks of any color.

"You've told me about your mother." His heart beat a heavy rhythm in his chest. "Now tell me about you. Tell me what you lost."

A tear broke free and traced a path to the corner of her mouth. He watched as she worked to form the words. When she spoke, he had to strain to hear.

"I lost…my father."

"And…?" he nudged with a quiet voice.

"My mother." Another tear fell.

"And?" he pushed again.

"Everything. I lost everything, too." Tears came in a constant stream now. "How could he have not known what his death would do to us?"

"He was a cop. He faced death every day."

"But this was different."

"Why?"

"Why? Because he had to be noble. He had to try to save his partner, and got himself killed."

"You blame him for that, don't you?"

"Damn straight. He had responsibilities. He had a wife and child to provide for—" She stopped.

"And you're pissed off that he chose Dexter over you."

"Yes." Her lips formed the silent admission.

A flicker of relief slipped through his chest. Her mother's collapse had prevented Elf from ever working all the way through her grief. Better twenty years late than never. "That's normal, you know."

"Is that supposed to make me feel better?"

He shrugged.

"Well, it doesn't." She scrubbed the tears from her cheeks. "I'll feel better when Marvin Dexter pays for what he did to my parents."

"And to you?"

She jammed her feet back into her pumps. "Yes. And to me. I admit it."

He blocked her from the door. "Where do you think you're going?"

"Shrink session is over. Thanks, Doc, but I have things to do."

He wouldn't let her go anywhere in her present frame of mind. "Revenge won't solve anything."

"Not revenge. Justice."

"You're going to see that Dexter gets justice?"

"It's about time that sonofabitch paid for his sins."

"I can't let you do that."

"Try and stop me." She feinted to the right. He caught her arm.

The handcuff ratcheting closed sounded loud in the room. She looked down at her wrist. "You're kidding."

"Never been more serious in my life." He put the other cuff around his wrist, hoping her anger would be short term.

"Get this off of me. You can't do this. It's unlawful detainment."

"That didn't stop you."

She jerked her wrist.

He pulled her close and wrapped his arm around her. "I'm sorry, Elf."

Angel stood stiff and silent in Cabrini's embrace. He had no idea how sorry he was going to be.

Did he really think he could stop her? She'd worked her entire career with one intention—bring her father's murderer to justice. That she hadn't expected it to be someone she knew didn't matter. The only thing that mattered was closing the case.

Cabrini cradled her head in his free hand, pressing her to his chest. For a breath, she almost gave in and relaxed. That's what he wanted. Maybe, on some level, she wanted to, too.

For one weak moment, she considered what it would mean to relax into his embrace. The day had given her a taste of what it could be like to work with someone, to have a partner to share things with and to stand at her back.

But that wasn't in the cards for her. She worked alone. No one, no matter how well-intentioned, would stop her from doing her job.

He pressed a kiss to her forehead. Longing, stronger than any she'd experienced, shot through her.

Why did he have to be so different? Why couldn't he have been like every man she'd ever dated? Then she could lose interest and go her way without wondering what it would be like.

He wouldn't be staying. As soon as he closed his case, he'd be gone. The thought should comfort her. There were no strings attached to their relationship.

Except, the fact that she considered what they had a relationship proved he was different.

She tried to pull away, but he held her close, running

his hand up and down her spine, coaxing tense muscles to relax.

How had she let him get so deep under her skin? She needed to get some distance. "How long do you plan on standing here?"

His arms loosened and he drew her back to the bed. She wanted to resist.

But not really. Not yet. The tiny voice came from deep inside. *Let him hold you.*

How much harm could it do?

Plenty.

She couldn't fight him. Not physically, anyway. She'd bide her time, lay the groundwork for her escape. When the opportunity presented itself, she'd take it.

He pulled her down to sit beside him on the edge of the bed. "I won't let you ruin your life."

"Ruin my life?" His words caught her by surprise.

"If you go after Dexter, that's what will happen."

"Your confidence in my abilities is almost… whelming."

He shifted on the mattress, turning to look at her. "I have no doubts about your abilities to take care of yourself. It's your intentions that worry me."

"I thought we covered that." She closed her eyes and sighed. "I intend to make Dex pay."

"How?"

"The same way my father paid."

"With his life." He crooked a finger under her chin.

Sitting near him, having him touch her, amounted to torture. She didn't want to look in his eyes, see the disapproval she heard in his voice.

He forced her to meet his gaze. Worse. Pity.

She jerked and looked away.

"Consider the consequences of your actions, Elf. If you're successful—"

"The world will be a better place."

"You'll be no different from Dexter. He stole your parents from you. If you kill him, you'll steal yourself from your mother."

"What concern is that of yours? What makes you think you even have any say in the matter?"

"I care about you, Elf." He laced his fingers through hers. "I'd like to think that counts for something."

"You care. Gee, that's nice." Bitterness tinged her voice. "So you're going to save me from myself. You come in here, help solve a twenty-year-old murder and then you leave. I suppose I should be grateful."

"No."

"When you go back to Boston, to your nice, big family and your nice, steady job, you can file this whole experience under CF, for Crazy Family. Or maybe it really stands for—"

He stopped her with a kiss.

It was a full-frontal, all-out kiss, not his usual, gradual, nibbling buildup that drove her crazy. Her breath caught in her throat.

Thoughts of him leaving hurt too much. She wanted to lose herself in his kisses.

Damn him. Damn his kisses.

From the first time she tailed him, she knew he would be trouble. It never occurred to her just how bad it could get.

She needed to save herself.

His free hand cupped her cheek and he threaded his fingers into her hair as he tilted her head back. His breath feathered across her neck, raising goose bumps and setting off alarms.

Two could play at this game. He thought he could distract her with some foreplay? She'd show him distraction.

She allowed him to lead, playing along with his love-making. Neither whispered a word. No endearments. No promises that couldn't be kept.

He slipped his hand beneath her blouse and caressed a path to her breast. Shivers followed in the wake of his touch.

She worked her hand beneath his shirt, mimicking his progress. Beneath her hand, his skin tightened, his nipple pebbled.

He nipped at her lips, her neck, her collarbone, pulling her over him as he laid out on the mattress.

Somewhere between his first kiss and her current position on top of him, her intentions shifted.

This wasn't supposed to happen. She was independent, a loner. Men held no interest for her.

Men didn't. But this man did.

He cared for her. Such a weak emotion compared to everything she felt.

For the first time, she wished she knew the secret to making a man fall in love. When he left, she wanted to be more than just a fond memory, an entertaining interlude in his life.

She wanted him to look back and remember what they'd had, wonder what they could have been.

Partners. Equals. In everything.

Her fingers flexed and her nails grazed across his skin. His breath shuddered and an answering surge ran to her belly. She pushed away until she straddled him.

His cuffed hand followed hers as she undid his buttons and pushed his shirt out of the way. He used his free hand to unbutton her blouse.

He sat up, catching her around the waist as he pushed her skirt over her thighs. She worked at his belt. Their hands tangled, exciting each other and themselves, as they undid zippers and pushed fabric out of the way.

All the while, he kissed her and she kissed back. Tasting hunger, fueling arousal, driving need.

He pressed a foil packet into her hand. She ripped it open and rolled the sheath in place. Light glinted off the handcuffs still holding them together.

"Remember?" His rough whisper raced over her skin. "The rest stop."

She closed her eyes and nodded, not trusting her voice. She remembered. Every thought, every longing, every dream.

This was as close as she could hope for any of those half-formed wishes to become a reality.

He would leave and she would live with the memories of what they'd almost had.

Her hands covered his as he grasped her hips and guided her home. The soft jingle of the handcuffs reminded her of their presence.

She smiled as she swallowed back her tears. Somehow, it seemed fitting to be handcuffed to the man she'd come to love as she told him goodbye.

Chapter 16

Frank woke to the sound of a handcuff closing. "What the devil…?"

He couldn't have slept for more than a few minutes, yet, somehow, Elf had managed to get out of her half of the cuffs and attach it to the bed frame.

She stepped back, out of his reach. For one brief instant, she looked like she might apologize. Then her expression settled into a mask.

He pushed into a sitting position. "What are you playing at?"

"Nothing. It's just…" She looked away, took a deep breath. "We have different opinions of how to proceed on this case. I'm not inclined to negotiate, so—"

"A preemptive strike." He tugged his shirt together and managed to fight one button through the corresponding hole before he gave up. "I don't believe this."

She shrugged and turned away from him. The stiff line of her back contradicted her casual gesture.

This was not the aftermath he'd expected. Of course, he hadn't expected to make love when they got to his room, hadn't intended to get carried away when he kissed her. Her response had caught him by surprise.

A sick feeling settled in his gut.

She unzipped the skirt he'd pushed out of the way as they'd made love and slid it over her hips. It fell to the floor, revealing her naked backside.

His body reacted, even as his brain tried to deny the suspicions taking root. "You played me?"

The possibility came close to choking him. Could he have been that wrong about her?

Without a word, she shed the rest of her clothes, then rummaged in her briefcase.

No, not this time, not Elf.

She wanted him to think it hadn't meant anything. But her body told a different story. A soft flush tinted her skin.

"It's not going to work a second time." He wouldn't let her do this.

She looked over her shoulder but didn't meet his eyes. "What?"

"Using your body to distract me."

She shook out the bundle she'd dug from her briefcase. "I only needed the once."

He watched as she pulled on a sport bra and leggings. "Why?"

"Isn't it obvious?" She stomped into her running shoes.

"What I'm asking is, why cheapen yourself like that?"

The color drained from her face. She refused to look at him, focusing, instead, on her gun as she clipped it inside her waistband.

"I think I deserve an answer."

"Why? Because you think I was a virgin?" She opened his closet door and pulled out one of his white dress shirts. "Like that gives you some special rights?"

"*Think?* Uh-uh." Anger laid a sharp edge on his tone. "I *know,* and you aren't going to take that away. Even without the sex, what we had was different, special. And I want to know why you're doing your damnedest to destroy it."

"Don't you get it?" She slipped his shirt on and tied the tails in a loose knot at her waist, covering her revolver. "This is what I do."

He shook his head.

"Yes." She squared her shoulders and faced him. "I put on a disguise and play to people's expectations. They see what they want and I use that to get what I want." She held her arms wide. "This is who I am."

"No. Not this time. Not with me."

"We both knew from the start this would be short-term. Don't try to make it more than it could ever have been."

He couldn't deny that and it was his own damn fault. They never talked about the future, about what would happen after they closed the case.

The one thing he knew without question was that he wanted her to be a permanent part of his life. And she was about to walk out the door and leave him chained to the bed.

"What are you going to do?"

"Stop Dex."

"How?" He couldn't let her go after Dex alone. He'd tear the bed apart bare-handed if he had to. She was not going out the door without him.

She rested her hand at her waist, over her gun.

"Don't." Ice-cold dread settled in his chest. If the worst happened, her actions would haunt her for the rest of her life. "You're better than that."

Virgin in Disguise

"Am I?" Doubt darkened her eyes.

"Your mother believes so."

"My mother doesn't live in the real world."

"I do." He held out his free hand.

She turned away from him.

Her rejection hit him with the force of a bullet. This was a nightmare. Worse. At least if he slept, he might wake up and find her lying beside him. He'd tell her he loved her. Everything would be okay.

Instead, her drive for justice would destroy them.

Justice. Maybe that was the key.

He packed away his pain and took a deep breath. "Your father set out to put an end to Dexter's arson scam. He believed in the legal system enough to follow the rules."

"Look where it got him."

"This is your opportunity to prove him right. Honor Patrick Donovan's memory and finish the job his way—legally."

"What makes you think I'll have any better luck than he did?"

"You have something he didn't—me as backup."

She raised one eyebrow as she looked at his cuffed wrist.

"Present evidence to the contrary, I'm a good man to have at your back."

"So you keep telling me."

"Your mother knew you were headed for a face-off with Dex someday. She didn't want you to be alone. She's afraid she'll lose you, like she did your father."

"He underestimated Dex. I won't make the same mistake."

"Are you sure?" He needed her to see the similarities, see she really was headed down the same wrong path her father had taken. "Your father didn't want to believe Dexter was unredeemable. You've been fighting that same truth about him from the beginning."

"Yeah, well, I've seen the light."

"Your father went without backup. What are you planning on doing?"

She dug her fingers through her hair, leaving it spiked in every direction. "I'll have the element of surprise on my side."

"You think so? Like when he had the cabin blown up?"

"We've managed to stay ahead of him."

"Yes, *we* have." It wasn't much, but he'd take any opening he could get. "We make a good team." *C'mon Elf. Give us another chance.*

"How long is that going—" The ring of her cell phone interrupted her. She frowned at the display window and flipped the phone open. "Mom?"

Her eyes widened and she mouthed something that looked like "Omaha." "When?" she asked aloud.

She dug out the handcuff key and threw it in his direction as she peppered her caller with a series of questions. He managed to pull on a pair of jeans and dodge her pacing circuit of the room. Getting a read on what had her near panic proved more difficult.

She ended the call. "We've got to get out of here."

"What happened?"

"Corie was mowing the lawn. When she came in, Mom had disappeared."

"No sign of her in the neighborhood?" He pulled a T-shirt over his head.

"No. There was a message on the answering machine, from Dex, asking me to meet him at some warehouse. Corie seemed to think…"

"What?" He strapped on his ankle holster and tied his shoes.

"Corie said Mom has been talking about the past a

lot the last few days. She's confusing the past and present. Dex's message said something about Dad. Mom might think she's going to meet him."

"Then we've got a starting point for our search."

"No." She closed her eyes and he wanted to shield her from the raw pain etched across her face. "When Corie tried to replay the message, to get the address, she hit the wrong button."

"Erased?"

She nodded.

"Your mother can't have gotten too far without her car—"

"She took Rusty."

Angel's eyes burned as she stared at her cell phone.

She needed to call someone. Who? Her fingers trembled. *Calm down. Think.* She breathed in and out—deep, calming breaths.

"How long has she been missing?" Cabrini stood beside her.

"Corie didn't know. Maybe an hour. She was outside at least that long." She tried swallowing to dislodge her heart from where it had stuck in her throat.

The room closed in and she paced off the narrow width. "Other than doctor's appointments and an occasional weekend drive, Mom almost never leaves the house. When she does, either Corie or I drive."

She stopped and faced him across the room. He had no obligation to help her, especially after what she'd just done. She had no right to ask and wouldn't blame him if he refused. "I need wheels."

"Not a problem."

"No?" A few minutes ago, they were through working together. She'd done her best to burn that bridge. Now... "You'll let me use your car?"

"On one condition."

She needed his car and would go along with just about anything.

"I go with you."

Anything but that. It hurt too much, loving him and knowing they had no future. She wanted to get away from him.

She needed to find her mother.

Her heart finally came loose from her throat and fell all the way to the pit of her stomach.

In the battle of need and want, need won. This time. "Let's go."

She followed him to the street where he'd parked his navy blue Ford Taurus. After weeks of tailing him, she recognized the car before he said anything.

"Where should we start?" Cabrini's question gave her something to focus on for a brief moment.

She gave her scalp a furious itching. "We could cruise through some of the streets between here and home, but I have a bad feeling about what kind of luck we'll have."

As Cabrini drove, she searched, twisting and turning to look down cross streets, praying she'd catch a glimpse of her car.

"Do you think she's in danger?" Cabrini put her shadowy fear into words.

"She hasn't driven in years. If she makes it to wherever she's going, she'll have survived the worst of it."

"What about Dexter?"

"No. He won't hurt her."

"She hired The Diamond Group. If he makes the connection, you don't think he'd perceive her as a threat to his plans?"

"Not Mom." Fading light made it difficult to distinguish vehicles from any distance. She gave up trying.

"He's already proved the lengths he'll go to to protect her. We're the threat he's concerned about."

"How do you think he'll react when she shows up instead of us?"

"I don't know. If he's preoccupied with her, it might work to our advantage."

"Same holds true in reverse. He could use her presence as a shield, protect himself from us."

Frustration gnawed at her nerves. She wanted to scream, to beat on something, do anything, as long as she could be in control for a few minutes. "This is useless. We're driving in circles and getting nowhere."

He gave her hand a squeeze. "Too bad we don't have a tracking device on Rusty."

She thumped her forehead with her hand. "Mush for brains," she mumbled.

Cabrini may have been joking, but he was closer than he could have guessed. "I installed a radio tracker last year." She dialed her phone again.

"Way to go, Elf."

Her buddy in the cold case division picked up on the third ring. "McDonough."

"George, it's Angel. Are you on today?"

"I'm always on, you know that. What's happening?"

"My car's gone AWOL and I need your help."

"You know I'll do anything for you, but it'd be quicker to call the regular number."

"I think my mom took Rusty."

A soft whistle came over the phone. "Yeah, I can see where that would be a concern. Does she even have a driver's license anymore?"

"That'd be the least of the problems. I don't want the cops to descend on her. It'd push her over the edge."

"Gotcha."

"Can you activate the tracker and call me when you have the location? Without alerting the whole precinct?"

"No problem, kiddo. I'm on it. I'll call as soon as I get something you can use."

"You're the best. Thanks." She disconnected.

Cabrini rolled to a stop at a traffic light. "Now what?"

She leaned her head back and closed her eyes. "We wait for him to call with the location of the car. Then we hope Mom's somewhere nearby and safe."

"Who was he?"

"A buddy."

"That much I gathered. I'm not trying to steal a source, Elf. I'd just like to know who's in the game."

"George McDonough. We met in college, had some criminal justice classes together, kept in touch."

"Now?"

"He works cold cases."

"You trust him?"

"He's a good man."

"Do you trust him?"

"He's been able to provide some leads on different cases for me."

"What does he get in return?"

"A pretty good closure rate."

"That's all?" The light changed and he drove through the intersection.

"It's to everyone's benefit to get some of the old cases settled."

"Is your father's murder one of those cases?"

"Yes." She glanced at her watch, wishing George would call back. Not nearly enough time had elapsed yet. But it was the top of the hour.

She turned on the radio, tuning in to the all-news KNOW. The latest report filled the silence and eliminated conversation, at least for a few minutes.

Very few possible conversation topics held any interest at the moment. Cabrini had a bad habit of making her talk about things she'd just as soon leave unexplored. Any subject he might bring up would, no doubt, force her to unwanted introspection.

He turned the radio off. "I've been thinking, Elf."

"That'll get you in trouble."

She could just make out his grin in the evening light. "Be that as it may... What I'm wondering is why your cold case buddy feeds you information when you're a bounty—bond enforcer, not a P.I.?"

"After he'd been on the force for a few years, he started to hear rumors about my father's case. We'd talked about it a lot in college, so he passed on what he could. Primarily, he lets me know of any leads. Sometimes things spill over into other cases. If I can help out, no harm done."

"Still, you're not a licensed investigator."

"Even on a straight bail jumper, I do plenty of investigation. It's not a foreign territory to me." He couldn't be questioning her ability, could he? "Information I'm able to pass back to George tends to be more reliable than that of the typical private citizen who might call a lead into the tip line."

"Do you like the investigating part?"

"Sure." She studied him. What game was he playing at? "Thinking of taking up career counseling, Cabrini?"

"Just wondering what you're going to do when we solve your father's murder."

Oh. Her brain froze on the thought for a second. "I never gave it much consideration." And now that he'd planted the question, she couldn't escape thinking about it. After all these years, what would she do? "There's no reason for me to not continue what I'm doing."

"Is there any motivation to continue?"

"Right now, all I'm motivated to do is find my mother and make sure she's safe. There'll be plenty of time to worry about the rest of my life later."

"Spoken like a true ostrich."

She ignored him, but she couldn't ignore the question. If ever she hoped for a timely phone call, now would be it.

On cue, her cell rang. The exchange matched that of the police department. "Donovan."

"It's George."

"You've got it?"

"Yeah, and I'm not liking what I see. You know that warehouse fire last week?"

"On the north side?"

"That's the one. Rusty's sitting on the front doorstep of what's left."

"We're on our way."

"Angel, be careful. That place isn't safe."

"I know. Thanks."

"What you don't know is they're going to announce the preliminary results of the investigation tomorrow."

A chill traced over her skin at his tone. "What are they going to say?" She held her breath.

"There are similarities between this fire and others. Including some old cases in my files. They believe they're related."

"Serial arson." She met Cabrini's questioning look.

"And homicide." George's voice disappeared behind the rushing in her ears.

Arson. Homicide. And her mother parked at the scene.

Frank covered Elf's shaking hand with his. She never noticed when he pried the cell phone from her grip. All color had drained from her face, and she seemed to struggle for each breath she took.

He flipped the turn signal and pulled to the side of the street.

"Don't stop." Panic sharpened her voice. "Why are you stopping?"

"Because you're about to hyperventilate."

"I'm fine. I'll be fine. We need to get to the warehouse."

"We will, but first you have to tell me what your friend told you."

Between her hyperspeed recap of the details and what he'd been able to glean from listening to her side of the conversation, he didn't like the picture forming.

"Will you get this heap back on the road. We need to get to that warehouse."

"What do you think we're going to be able to do once we're there?"

"I don't know, but we need to get there."

"We need a plan."

"We can come up with one while you're driving."

"I'm not liking this, Elf. Not one bit."

"You think I am? My mother is there." Her voice cracked.

"All the more reason to proceed with caution. We don't want to put her in danger."

"Just drive. Can you do that? Can you just drive? We can talk all you want on the way there. Please."

He studied her face for a moment, then shifted the car into gear. "Fine. Where are we going?" If he wanted to protect her, the best way to start would be helping to keep her mother safe.

She directed him to an area north of downtown Minneapolis, where warehouses mingled with railroad tracks.

"What do you think we'll find there?"

"I'm praying my mother sitting in my car."

"Okay, that's the best-case scenario. What's the worst?"

She took a deep breath and let it out on a long sigh. "I'm not sure how much of the structure survived the fire. She may be walking around inside the ruins."

"There's a flashlight in the glove box. We'll need it if we have to follow her."

Elf dug in the compartment and pulled out the heavy-duty flashlight. She clicked it on and off a couple of times, making sure the batteries had some juice. "You just have the one?"

"One is all we'll need. We're not splitting up."

In the dim light, he could see the white of her knuckles as she clutched the flashlight.

He squeezed her hand, trying to relay some comfort. "How much farther?"

"We're almost there. Another block—there."

He pulled into the parking lot and got out of the car. He met Elf by the passenger door.

The scene of the burned-out warehouse looked straight out of a nightmare. The roof sagged in some sections; broken windows glittered in the pale moonlight. The stench of soot and burned chemicals hung in the air.

No streetlights functioned in the immediate vicinity. The moon barely gave off enough light for them to pick their way through the debris scattered around the pavement. As they neared the building, he could make out an indistinct blob that could be a car.

The flashlight came to life. Elf swept its beam across the shape. A side mirror reflected and magnified the light as it bounced away.

"Cheyenne." Elf's soft oath came to him in the stillness.

"So it's the worst-case scenario. Maryam's wandering somewhere inside?"

"Worse than the worst-case. She's not alone." She threaded her fingers through his and pulled him to the side. The flashlight shone on a black Lincoln Town Car.

"Any idea whose car that is?"

"It belongs to Dex."

Chapter 17

Angel forced herself to take even breaths, and pushed back the nausea rolling up her throat. She tried to make sense of the evidence in front of her, but nothing came.

Why here? Why now? In spite of everything she had learned, some small part of her still insisted on finding alternative explanations. She wanted to believe Dex had joined their search for Maryam, and somehow tracked her down first.

Except the position of the two cars made it clear he'd arrived first.

She approached the Town Car and peered inside. Neat, orderly, not a scrap of paper, nothing to indicate if he'd been in a rush to get to the site.

Cabrini caught her arm as he walked past. He pulled her to the building entrance. The door, barricaded by several boards, hung open just enough to let an adult squeeze through. Yellow crime-scene tape fluttered from the charred door frame like party streamers.

He wrapped one hand in the tape and pushed the door farther open.

They stopped just inside the building. The beam of her flashlight danced off broken glass and soot-darkened walls. Water still pooled beside collapsed shelves. Piles of debris lay everywhere.

Some creature scuttled through the darkness. She swung the flashlight in a wild arc, trying to spot the source.

Cabrini motioned for silence as he eased the flashlight from her death grip. She shook the blood back into her fingers. He crouched to study the floor around them. When he stood, she caught the glint of his Beretta in his hand.

He pulled her back to the door and outside. She wanted to protest, but the grim expression on his face changed her mind. "What's the matter?"

"Call your friend." He pressed her cell phone into her hand. When had he taken it from her? "Tell him a SWAT team might be a good idea."

That snapped her attention into sharp focus. "What did you see?"

"More footprints than I can account for. There are at least two people other than Dex and Maryam in there. Maybe more. I'm going to see if I can find anything else out. You call McDonough."

He disappeared around the corner of the building. His absence chilled her. For the first time in her professional career, she admitted what an advantage there was in having a partner.

She made the call. Cabrini returned as she finished. "He can't guarantee a SWAT team, but units are on their way. We're supposed to stay out here until they arrive."

"Right." He turned and headed back into the building.

If you didn't already own it, you just won my heart.
She followed him.

They didn't use the flashlight this time, not wanting
to reveal their position before they were ready. Cabrini
led the way through the building, guided by some faint
path he seemed able to discern. All she could see was
dark. All she could hear was the pounding of her heart.

She eased her gun out of her waistband as they approached a large, open space. Indistinct voices echoed
in the air, unanchored in any reality she could identify.

An eerie tableau unfolded ahead of them. Cloud-
chased moonlight filtered in from the collapsed roof.
Two figures stood in the center of the open area.

Dex, his hands in the air, faced her mother. She
clutched a revolver with both hands and held an unwa-
vering aim on his chest.

Angel tried to step forward, but Cabrini held her
back. He leaned close and whispered in her ear. "Patience, Elf. I'll check on the other footprints, see if I can
neutralize them. You stay here, find out as much as you
can."

She wanted to protest, wanted to go to her mother
and stop her before the nightmare took a turn for the
worse. But Cabrini was right. They needed to eliminate
as many variables as possible before making their move.

He disappeared into the unlit expanse of the warehouse. She sidled as close as possible while staying
hidden in the deep shadows.

"If only you had married me." Dex's voice carried
to her. "You should have. Then none of this would have
happened."

"Marry you?" The disbelief in her mother's voice
echoed her own.

"Is it really so hard to imagine? Maryam, I could
have given you so much more than Patrick. I would have

given you everything." He held out one hand as he stepped toward her. "I loved you."

"Loved? No. You coveted." Her mother took a step back. "You saw what Patrick and I had and you wanted it for yourself."

"Maryam, please." Dex's voice changed, his tones calming and conciliatory. "Think about what you're doing."

"I've done nothing but think for the last twenty years."

"You've been ill—"

"No, I haven't, and you know it. My 'fragile mental state' was all your doing. You and the kindly Dr. Sanders."

Angel's breath caught. What…?

"You're imagining things." Dex tried to reason with her. "That's what prompted Sanders to put you on the medication. Your new doctor should have talked to me. I could have explained it to her."

"I'm sure you would have. Just like you explained to Sanders the importance of keeping me in a drugged fog. Robbing me of my husband wasn't enough, Marvin? You had to steal my life, as well?"

Angel swallowed a sob. Her mother had known all these years, and had been powerless to do anything.

"I know you blame me for Patrick's death. I blame myself."

"If I thought you had a conscience, I might believe you."

"Things could have been different. Patrick didn't even have to participate. All he had to do was turn a blind eye."

"To your corruption and blackmail? How could you ever think he'd go along with that? He was a cop. He took pride in everything that meant. You were never anything like him."

Dex stiffened. He clenched his hands and took a step toward her mother.

Angel tensed, slipped her finger onto her gun's trigger and held her breath.

Maryam backed up, maintaining her distance from Dex. "Patrick considered you his best friend. When he realized what you were doing, it nearly destroyed him."

"It didn't have to be that way." Dex slid his hands into his pants pockets.

"True, you could have turned yourself in. Instead, you killed your partner." Her mother took a deep breath and steadied the gun, aiming at Dex's chest. "It's fitting, don't you think, that now you face his gun."

"You don't want to do this."

"What are my alternatives? Let you walk?"

"There's always the private investigator you hired."

Some of the determination left Maryam's face. "How did you find out about him?"

"You forget how connected everything is in life. Of course I know about him. I sent Angela after him. It's only a matter of time before she brings him to me. Like her father, she's very good at what she does."

The compliment, had it come from anyone else, would have thrilled Angel. Now, in this place, under these circumstances, it bore the taint of betrayal, and she wanted nothing to do with it.

"My daughter is a very determined woman. Since the day she understood about Patrick's death, she's been driven to find his killer. It's the one thought I managed to hold all these years, the one thing I was able to pass on to her. Have you any idea what a horrible legacy that is?" She cocked the gun. "I won't see her destroyed by you."

Angel couldn't wait any longer. *Where was Cabrini?* With a prayer that he would come through and watch her back, she stepped from the shadows. "Mom, don't."

* * *

Frank found the first of Dexter's men within a minute of leaving Elf. He took him down, and had him bound and gagged without making a sound.

The need to get back to Elf drove him. She'd taken some big emotional hits over the last few days. He couldn't do anything to lessen the impact, but he wanted to be there to help her hold the pieces together.

He'd nearly reached the entrance of the building before he found their second shadow watching the door they'd come through.

In a matter of seconds, the man was no longer a concern. Frank stood over him, adrenaline buzzing through his veins, sensitizing every nerve ending, magnifying every reaction.

A shuffling noise alerted him to the presence of someone else, an instant before a hand clamped on his shoulder. He spun around, trapped the attacker's arms between their bodies and pulled back his fist.

Dex moved, and Angel swung her gun up to aim at his heart. "If you so much as twitch an eyelid, I will shoot, and damn the consequences."

He froze in place. Angel lowered her gun and faced her mother. "Mom, please. Don't do this."

Maryam shook her head. "You don't know what he did."

"I opened the safe-deposit box. We know enough."

"He deserves to die."

"You won't get an argument from me on that one."

"Then why shouldn't I?"

She understood the question in her soul. Looking in her mother's eyes, she knew the answer, as well. "Because that's not how Dad would have done it. He trusted the system to work." She hadn't wanted to listen to Cabrini. Now, saying the words herself, she realized the truth in them. "It's not how he'd want us to handle it."

Her mother took a shaky breath. "I miss him so much."

"I know. Me, too." She slipped her gun into her waistband and eased a step closer to her mother.

"I know your father wanted to see justice. I'm not willing to risk it failing him again."

"It won't fail. We won't let it."

Maryam studied her gun. "It would be so easy. A simple squeeze of the trigger. I'm close enough—he's an easy target."

"If you do, you'll be no better than he is. You lose. And I lose. He stole my father. I don't want to lose my mother. Not again." She edged closer and held out her hand. "Please, Mom."

Tears spilled down her mother's cheeks. She handed the service revolver to Angel.

Relief sapped her muscles, leaving her knees shaking. She tucked the gun into the back of her waistband and hugged her mother.

"Well done, Elf." Cabrini's voice triggered a cascade of emotions.

She hadn't wanted to believe his assertion that they were stronger together. But he'd been right. Because she knew he was covering the perimeter and keeping them safe, she'd been able to focus on her mother and getting that portion of the situation under control.

He stepped out of the shadows on the opposite side of the clearing and joined them in the moonlight. His presence energized her confidence that they could handle anything, as long as they were together.

She released her mother, but stayed by her side.

"Let's see how these fit the councilman." Cabrini held out his set of handcuffs.

"I have a better idea." A woman's voice came from the darkness behind them.

Angel searched the inky shadows of the warehouse, but couldn't see anyone. Then a figure moved and separated from the deeper black.

"Corie?" The lighting had to be playing tricks on her. What would her mother's companion be doing here?

The figure stepped farther into the open. The semi-automatic pistol in her hand gleamed in the dull light. "None other."

"What are you doing here? What's with the gun?"

"I thought there might be a little trouble, so I came to lend a hand."

"We've got everything under control."

"Correction. You *had* control. Now you don't, I do."

"What are you doing?" True fear traced cold fingers down Angel's back.

"Exactly what I was hired to do—watch out for Dex's investments." Corie pointed to Angel's waist. "Let's start with the guns, shall we? Put them both on the floor and push them over here."

For a heartbeat, she calculated her chances of getting off a clean shot at Corie. But her mother stood too close, and Corie had her gun aimed at Maryam. Angel laid both guns on the ground and gave them a weak nudge.

"You, too, lover-boy." Corie didn't shift her aim.

Cabrini laid his gun on the floor and pushed it in Corie's direction. It stopped close to the revolvers.

"Very good. Now. About those handcuffs. Why don't you go ahead and slip one on."

When Cabrini closed the manacle on his right wrist, Corie nodded. "Your turn, Angel. Put the other cuff on your right wrist."

Angel hesitated. Cuffing their right wrists together

limited their range of motion. Neither could move effectively without being taken off balance by the other. But it would leave Cabrini's dominant hand free.

"That wasn't a request," Corie said.

The cuff ratcheted closed. Angela and Cabrini stood facing each other. "Good thing we have practice," he said, for her ears only.

The warmth of his hand, so close to hers, calmed her. She wasn't alone. They could do this together.

"There now. Isn't this cozy? Everyone together, at last." Corie turned to Dex. "Now we can finally finish the plan."

"What plan?" Angel twisted around to look at Dex. Cabrini moved with her.

Corie answered for Dex. "There's really only one obstacle to Dex's campaign—an investigation too far into the past might turn up some less than exemplary behavior. Those who benefited wouldn't say anything. But there were a couple who couldn't be controlled that way."

Cabrini snorted. "Yeah, I can see where murder, arson, insurance fraud and blackmail might hang a shadow over a political career."

"Exactly. The best way to eliminate a problem is to go straight to the root. In this case, those who might have proof of such behavior but weren't vulnerable to control."

"So he engineered a connection between you and Mom and me." Angel looked at Dex. "All these years, you've just been waiting for the right opportunity?"

"It wasn't particularly hard." Again, Dex left the answering to Corie.

"Interesting." Cabrini glanced between Corie and Dex, then turned to Angel. "Don't you think?"

"Now that you mention it, yes." She followed his lead, hoping they were on the same train of thought.

"What?" Corie demanded.

"You know what he's doing, don't you?" Cabrini asked her.

"What are you talking about?"

"The councilman is letting you do all the talking." His answer echoed what she'd noticed.

He shifted his position to face Corie. In the process, he got a step closer to the guns, and his body became a shield between her gun and Angel.

"So? We're partners. We've been working toward this moment for years now. Why shouldn't I talk?"

"It's not so much that you shouldn't talk." Angel took a turn to do a little maneuvering and draw Corie's attention. She twisted around and nudged Cabrini over a step. He now stood between her mother and Corie. "It's that he isn't talking at all. A suspicious person might think he had a reason for that."

Corie tried to brush off their tactic. "Neither of you is making any sense."

"It's like this." Cabrini picked up the thread and continued. "You spill the plans, talk about the conspiracy, the years of planning, everything."

"And then something happens." Angel said.

"Like, we got word to the police before we came in here, and they show up." His right hand jerked, tugged their cuffed wrists.

"Only, Councilman Dexter never actually said anything." Angel infused her voice with mock sympathy to cover the hope flickering to life. "It was all just the ravings of a crazy person."

"He's as much of a victim as everyone else."

Angel nodded. "Poor Dex. The victim of a stalker who went too far."

"You're wrong."

"Really?"

"Tell them, Marvin. Tell them how you promised this would finish everything." Corie stalked to his side. "How, once these three were eliminated, there'd be no one left who knew about the past."

He remained silent.

Corie spun and paced back to them. "This doesn't prove anything."

"No, of course it doesn't." Angel spoke in a soft tone. "Besides, he failed to consider a few other details."

Cabrini answered Corie's questioning look. "There's the evidence we found. Pictures and audiotape from twenty years ago that prove just how dirty a cop Marvin Dexter was."

"And let's not forget our ace in the hole."

Angel's statement got a rise from Dex. He still didn't say anything, but he did snap to attention.

"Right." Cabrini smiled. "Your buddy working in the cold case division."

She nodded. "Who heard the rumors, but could never prove anything."

"There's someone else?" Corie stalked back to Dex. "You promised. You said these three, and then it would be done."

"He was right about one thing." A man's voice came from the shadows to their left. Corie and Dex swung around as a man stepped into the light. "It is done."

"No!" Corie raised her gun.

Angel grabbed for her mother as Cabrini scooped one of the guns from the floor. He swung around in front of them, and had his weapon trained on Corie when she pulled the trigger.

Chapter 18

The single gunshot whistled by Frank's ear and crashed into the darkness.

A riot of shouts flooded the area. Black-garbed figures rushed in from all sides, surrounding them and taking command.

Three members of the SWAT team took control of Dexter and Corie, searching, cuffing and Mirandizing them. Others fanned out to complete their search for any more of Dexter's men.

Through all the controlled chaos, Frank picked out Elf's voice. She stood at his back, repeating assurances to her mother that everything was okay. Her right hand clung to his.

George McDonough, the leader of the police team, trotted over and unlocked their cuffs. "Well, that didn't go quite the way we expected."

Elf's hand slipped from Frank's as she turned around to face McDonough. "You found us."

"With a little help from your friend."

She turned a questioning look to Frank. "I ran into them while taking care of Dexter's watchdogs."

"Ran into us. That's a nice way of putting it." George rubbed his jaw.

Frank shrugged off the comment. A slightly bruised police detective didn't concern him as much as Elf did. She looked half-shell-shocked. "Would it be all right if Angela took her mother home? You can get their statements tomorrow, can't you?"

"Good idea. I'll get someone to drive them home." McDonough went off to recruit a driver for them.

"I'll take care of things here." He brushed her hair smooth and pressed a kiss to her forehead. "Take care of your mom."

They needed time, and that was the one thing he could give them.

After she left, McDonough returned. "So you're the guy who's been driving Angel nuts?"

He smiled. "The condition is mutual."

McDonough nodded. "It looks like she's finally met her match."

"I doubt she sees it that way."

"Not yet, maybe. She's been so focused on making a living and solving Patrick's murder, she'll need a little time to adjust, find her new direction. I hope you're a patient man."

"I can be, when the situation calls for it. Like this one."

"Good to hear." McDonough clapped him on the back. They headed for the exit.

"How long have you known Dexter was guilty?"

McDonough sighed. "We never had anything solid— only rumors and suspicions. There was a report filed with Internal Affairs but nothing happened."

"The corruption went deeper?" Frank glanced toward the parking lot, wondering if he'd let Angel and her mother leave too soon. And unprotected.

"We've had our share of bad cops." McDonough shook his head. "But that wasn't the case. Our problem was a lack of evidence, pure and simple."

"The filing officer didn't have anything?"

"Never found out. He was killed in the line of duty just a couple of weeks after Patrick. IAD did the best they could with what they had, but it wasn't enough to take to the D.A."

"Will it be enough now?"

"Thanks to her help, and yours, we'll have more than enough."

McDonough stepped into the cool night air. "You'll testify if we need you?"

"Of course." He turned to the detective and held out his hand. "If you'll excuse me, I have a report of my own to file, and a few loose ends to tie up."

Two days later, Frank stood on the front step of the Donovan home. The scent of the freshly mown front yard filled the air. A lawn mower engine hummed somewhere behind the house.

He adjusted his tie and buttoned his suit jacket. The clothes fit his role as a member of a first-class private investigation firm. Putting on the wardrobe alleviated some of the jitters.

Not that he had anything to be nervous about. All he had to do was meet with his client and wrap up the case.

Right. The case provided a convenient excuse to be there, nothing more.

For the past two days, he'd spent most of his time thinking of Elf, trying to come up with a strategy to get them together. Permanently.

He felt naked. The freshly shaved jaw, exposed for the first time in nearly three months, didn't help.

Would she like it?

The door opened and his heart skidded to a stop.

Maryam Donovan studied him from behind the screen door. They hadn't really met the night of Dexter's arrest, so he didn't expect her to recognize him.

"Mrs. Donovan, I'm Frank Cabrini from The Diamond Group." He pulled his ID from his inside jacket pocket and held it up for her to see.

She studied if for a moment, then looked at him. "You were there the other night?"

"Yes, ma'am. I—"

"Clean up rather nicely." She opened the screen door. "Come in."

He crossed the threshold. A quick once-over revealed a neat house, with lots of windows and sunlight. And no sign of the daughter of the house.

He released a quiet sigh, whether of relief or disappointment, he couldn't say.

Maryam led him to the living room. He walked the perimeter, taking in the details. Books lay on side tables, ready to be picked up at the next opportunity. The television murmured in the background. On the mantel, a large photo of a man in police uniform held the place of honor. Several other photos, casual snapshots, showed the same man with younger versions of Maryam and Angela Donovan.

"My husband." Maryam stood beside him. She traced Patrick Donovan's jaw with a finger. "He's finally at peace, thanks to you."

"Your daughter did most of the work."

"Yes, that would be Angel. She always took responsibility very seriously. I'm afraid my situation put an early end to her childhood." She faced him. "You've had an...adventurous time with my daughter."

He smiled and shook his head. "That would be one way to describe it. I'd like to spend some time with her when we aren't being chased."

The back door opened. He turned at the sound and his heart thudded in his belly.

Maryam looked him over with an appraising eye. "Perhaps you should discuss those intentions with her?"

Angel opened the refrigerator door and soaked up the cool air. The obligatory run had been bad enough. Mowing the lawn on top of that deserved some sort of reward.

The Godiva ice cream in the freezer called to her. She grabbed the water jug and filled a glass. As soon as she cooled off and cleaned up, she'd take mom for a drive around the lake to Crema for some local, gourmet ice cream. They both deserved that.

She needed the distraction. Frank Cabrini had occupied more than a reasonable amount of her attention the past two days. Every time the phone rang or the doorbell chimed, her heart skidded to a stop.

The disappointment of his absence existed in a delicate balance with the excitement of her mother's recovery.

Her appointment with Dr. Brenna had done much to reassure her. While her mother still had some recovery issues, the future held the strong promise of a near-normal life.

She headed into the living room. "Mom, I finished the lawn. I'm crabby and crampy and as soon as I take a quick shower..." Her words trailed off when she spotted the stranger talking to her mother.

He was tall, like Cabrini, with broad shoulders like...

When had she started using Cabrini as a reference? She set her glass on a side table, straightened to her full height and pulled back her shoulders. "Mom? What did I tell you about answering the door?"

"I don't think Mr. Cabrini qualifies as a stranger, do you?"

"Cabrini?" She swallowed. He faced her, and a thousand memories flooded over her as she looked in his summer-sky eyes.

Acute awareness of her appearance heated her checks. Ragged, sweat-stained T-shirt and running shorts. Sweat-matted hair. Bits of grass sticking to her legs.

She broke eye contact and gave him a once-over. Well-tailored, charcoal pinstripe suit, crisp white shirt, red silk tie with a fine, black diamond pattern. He looked like a very successful businessman, a far cry from the day laborer she'd kidnapped. "You...shaved."

"I told him he cleaned up well."

"Mother!"

"Well he does."

"Even so—" She cut herself off, and her cheeks heated a couple hundred degrees more.

He rubbed his chin. "You approve?"

Approve? He couldn't possibly be concerned about her preference. That implied things like he cared about her opinion, and she had been anything other than an unwanted partner on a case, and that their days together meant even a fraction as much to him as they did to her.

No, he simply made polite conversation. A precursor to his real purpose for coming there. He'd been hired to do a job and now he wanted to wrap up the paperwork. "If you've come about the bill—"

"Angela!"

"—I hope your agency will take monthly payments.

It may take a while before I get enough money pulled together."

"The money isn't important."

She spun on her heel and stalked into the kitchen. Cabrini followed her. She lowered her chin and rested a clenched fist on her hip as she faced him. "I pay my debts."

"You don't owe anything."

"Don't owe? How does that work? You were on the case for two months. At the very least, you had expenses incurred. Plus time. I'm not sure how much your agency charges—" she gave him another, more pointed, once-over "—but I'm pretty sure it's not free."

"Consider it an audition."

"Audition? What are you talking about?"

"The Diamond Group wants to expand to the Midwest. Chicago was the initial choice, but I've convinced Kat Minneapolis has a lot of potential."

"Potential?" Her heart bounced from her throat to the pit of her stomach and back.

"We could really use someone with your talent."

We. Her heart settled back in place. "I see." Now her stomach sank. Damn him. She should have known. All along, his clothes were the giveaway. He was nothing but a suit, after all. He'd come on business.

Fine. She could deal with that. "How's the pay?"

"Top of the industry."

"Benefits?" If she was going to enter corporate America, she'd better get corporate perks. "Health? Dental? 401(k)?"

"All those." He smiled, and she discovered he had a deep dimple on each cheek.

Could she do this? "How long before the office is up and running?"

"I already started the process. A couple months should see everything in place."

Her heart and stomach met some place down around her knees. "Are you going to be the suit in charge?"

His eyes darkened, and he advanced on her. She retreated until she bumped against the counter.

He crowded way past her comfort zone. "This is as much a costume for me as anything you came up with while we were on the run." He brushed her cheek with the back of his fingers. "I'm not a suit. I'm not a cop." He cupped her hot, sweaty neck and pulled her closer.

Didn't he care that she was too sweaty and his suit was too good? She tried to hold him back.

He leaned in closer and took a deep breath. "Did I ever mention how much I love the scent of vanilla?"

Holy Sheboygan.

He nibble-kissed his way from the base of her neck to the corner of her mouth. "I'm not going anywhere, Elf. You're stuck with me for the duration."

A shiver raced down her back. "Duration of what?" He couldn't possibly mean…

"Our love. Which I'm expecting to be a long, long time. If you're willing to try."

She'd try to move Lake Mille Lacs, one teaspoon at a time, if he hauled water beside her. "Why, Mistah Cabrini." Her sigh slid into southern belle.

"Yes, Miss Elf?" He matched her accent.

She looked in his eyes, and knew. This man would see through any facade she tried to hide behind. The thought scared her. The prospect thrilled her.

Maryam Donovan slipped from her listening post at the kitchen door and returned to the living room. A smile lit her face as she picked up her husband's photograph. "It's going to be okay, Patrick. She's found her angel."

* * * * *

COMING NEXT MONTH

#1333 BENEATH THE SURFACE—Linda Turner
Turning Points

Crime reporter Logan St. John had sworn to protect Abby Saunders from her shady boss. But when Logan asked the innocent beauty on a date in order to investigate, he hadn't counted on falling for her! Soon a cover-up that could get them both killed was revealed, and Logan wondered if their newfound love would end before it even began....

#1334 RUNNING SCARED—Linda Winstead Jones
Last Chance Heroes

When a government official asked elite mercenary Quinn Calhoun to rescue Olivia Larkin from a ruthless dictator, he couldn't turn his back on the caring teacher. But an injury detained Cal and Livvie in the jungle, and passion flared between them. Could their growing love save them from the enemy, or would betrayal tear them apart?

#1335 SHATTERED VOWS—Maggie Price
Line of Duty

Lawman Brandon McCall had long since given up on his marriage to fiercely independent Tory DeWitt. Stubborn, beautiful Tory had never been willing to put her trust in Bran. But when he discovered an escaped convict's plan to exact revenge by harming Tory, he vowed to protect her at any cost—and win back her heart in the process.

#1336 DEADLY INTENT—Valerie Parv
Code of the Outback

Ryan Smith was the one man Judy Logan couldn't forget. After years away from her childhood crush, she now trusted him with the most important mission of her life—locating documents that could lead her to her family's fortune. But Ryan was keeping secrets, and the truth threatened to destroy their newfound love.

#1337 WHISPERS IN THE NIGHT—Diane Pershing
He'd been framed and sent to jail four years ago, but now Paul Fitzgerald was finally free—and getting close to Kayla Thomas was the only way to prove his innocence. But he hadn't counted on his attraction to the beautiful widow. He was determined to keep their relationship professional, until Kayla began receiving deadly threats, and he realized he would do anything to protect her.

#1338 DANGEROUS MEMORIES—Barbara Colley
Hunter Davis couldn't remember anything except an address in New Orleans and the face of a beautiful woman. So when he showed up at Leah Davis's door, she couldn't believe the husband who'd supposedly died five months ago was still alive. Could they rebuild their trust and find love again, or would Hunter's resurfacing memories cause Leah to lose him a second time?

SIMCNM1104